"You have to know by now that you're so much more than an assistant to me, Ainsley."

He tugged her a bit closer to him and used his fingertip to trace slow circles over her jawline. "Or did I not make that clear earlier when I kissed you?"

There was silence between them for a few long seconds.

"This may be off base," she said, "and please tell me if it is, but..." She touched his arm, slowly moving her hand until it was over his heart. "I think we should... I mean...do you want to just...you know...make love?"

"Is that what you want?" He picked up her hand from his chest, kissed it.

"Oh, yes."

He led her by the hand to the armchair. Taking a seat, he pulled her into his lap. A moment later, she leaned in for his kiss.

* * *

After Hours Attraction by Kianna Alexander
is part of the 404 Sound series.

Dear Reader,

Thanks so much for picking up *After Hours Attraction*! I hope you'll enjoy the ride as Ainsley, the responsible single mother, explores a relationship with her serious, slightly salty boss, Gage. These two have chemistry for days, but can they really make this cray workplace romance work? All will be revealed in the coming pages.

This is the second in my 404 Sound series, and if you love the glitz, glamour and drama of the Atlanta hip-hop scene, you're in the right place! If you haven't already, be sure to check out Eden and Blaine's story, *After Hours Redemption*.

As always, thanks so much for your support. It's very much appreciated.

All the best,

Kianna Alexander

KIANNA ALEXANDER

—

AFTER HOURS ATTRACTION

HARLEQUIN®

DESIRE™

Recycling programs
for this product may
not exist in your area.

ISBN-13: 978-1-335-23280-9

After Hours Attraction

Copyright © 2021 by Eboni Manning

This edition published by arrangement with Harlequin Books S.A.

For questions and comments about the quality of this book,
please contact us at CustomerService@Harlequin.com.

Harlequin Enterprises ULC
22 Adelaide St. West, 40th Floor
Toronto, Ontario M5H 4E3, Canada
www.Harlequin.com

Printed in U.S.A.

Like any good Southern belle, **Kianna Alexander** wears many hats: doting mama, advice-dispensing sister, fun aunt and gabbing girlfriend. She's a voracious reader, an amateur seamstress and occasional painter in oils. Chocolate, American history, sweet tea and Idris Elba are a few of her favorite things. A native of the Tar Heel state, Kianna still lives there while maintaining her collection of well-loved vintage '80s Barbie dolls.

For more about Kianna and her books, visit her website at authorkiannaalexander.com, or sign up for Kianna's Mailing List at authorkiannaalexander.com/sign-up/. You can also follow Kianna on social media: Facebook.com/kiannawrites, Twitter.com/kiannawrites, Instagram.com/kiannaalexanderwrites and Pinterest.com/kiannawrites.

Books by Kianna Alexander

Harlequin Desire

404 Sound

After Hours Redemption
After Hours Attraction

Visit her Author Profile page at Harlequin.com, or authorkiannaalexander.com, for more titles.

You can also find Kianna Alexander on Facebook, along with other Harlequin Desire authors, at Facebook.com/harlequindesireauthors!

To Atlanta, With Love

One

Tapping her fingers on the steering wheel in time with the Migos track flowing through her speakers, Ainsley Voss pulled up to the curb at Carter G. Woodson Academy, joining the long line of cars in the pickup lane. It was just before four thirty on a Friday afternoon, and she expected her eleven-year-old son, Cooper, to appear at any moment. Baseball practice always let out on time because Coach Tyler Rigsby was a stickler, with a family of his own to get home to.

A few minutes later, a stream of students who participated in various after-school enrichment activities offered at the academy began to stream out through the glass-paneled double doors. She scanned the crowd, smiling when her gaze landed on Cooper. His dirt-streaked baseball uniform looked like ten or twelve other kids', but his sideways cap and the bright orange backpack slung over his shoulder made him stand out among his peers. He was chatting with two of his teammates and didn't seem aware of her presence. She started to honk the horn but refrained when she remembered his whining the last time.

As the two other boys split off in different directions, Cooper looked her way. As he walked up and got into the car, she looked at him in the rearview. "Hey, honey."

"Hey, Ma." He threw his backpack onto the seat next to him and buckled his seat belt. "Practice was cool. I know you're gonna ask me that."

She chuckled. "Okay. What about the school day before that?"

"It was okay, too. I was bored out of my mind in Social Studies, but other than that…" He shrugged in that aloof adolescent way.

"Gotcha." She pulled away from the curb, inching along as the line of cars snaked toward the exit. Mindful of the signals from the crossing guard, she asked, "Anything else you want to tell me?"

After a few moments of silence, he said, "Yeah, actually. I need some stuff."

Ainsley wanted to sigh but held back. Whenever Cooper uttered the phrase *I need some stuff*, she knew she'd be bidding a sad farewell to a wad of cash. "Okay, I'm listening."

"Well, first, Coach says I need to replace my cleats ASAP since the soles are starting to come off. Then we have that field trip to DC to go to the Smithsonian in like two weeks. Did you forget?"

Making the left turn into city traffic, she cringed. "Sorry, Coop. I did forget. How much is it again?"

"It's like two hundred since we're staying overnight. And the money and the form were supposed to be turned in today, but Mrs. Rush gave me until Monday."

Damn. There goes girls' night out. "Is there anything else? Or is it just the cleats and the trip?" *Lord, please let that be it. My wallet is crying real tears.*

"It's only one more thing. Can you put some money on my streaming account? So I can download that new Lil Boosie? I promise I'll get the edited version."

Now, sitting in the thick of Atlanta traffic and mentally calculating how much of her hard-earned money she would soon part with, Ainsley felt the subtle throb begin in her right temple. "I guess I can put a few dollars on there, but that's really all I can spare, Coop."

"Oh yeah. Bryce asked if I could go to the movies tonight with him. Can I?"

Bryce Redford, son of her neighbors Fitz and Bebe Redford, was Cooper's best friend. The two boys were thick as thieves, studying together, playing sports together, and whiling away the hours with comic books and *Minecraft* marathons. She rubbed her temple, careful to keep her other hand on the wheel and her eyes on the road. "Yikes, Coop. I just dropped a stack on your semester tuition, plus those class valentines. I'm not made of money, sweetheart."

"I know, Mama. I'm sorry I need so much stuff." His tone sounded contrite.

Guilt squeezed her heart. "Don't worry about it, honey. I think you can go, but I'm not sure I can give you snack money."

"That's okay. Bryce is using his birthday money for snacks."

She sighed, unable to hold it back any longer. Sure, some of these things were wants, not needs, but she had no desire to get into that with him right now. Honestly, Cooper didn't ask for much. And he was a good kid. He studied hard, made good grades and stayed out of trouble—with the exception of the occasional youthful lapse in judgment. Southwest Atlanta held all kinds of trouble for a young boy his age to get into, and yet, despite his lack of a male figure in his life, he kept his nose clean. She was proud of him, and the whole reason she worked as hard as she did at 404 Sound recording studio was to make a good life for him.

By the time they got home, she was in full-blown headache mode. She entered the house and headed straight upstairs to the medicine cabinet for ibuprofen. Popping two of the pills with a handful of water from the sink, she flipped off the light and walked to her room to change. Once there, she kicked off her black suede pumps, then got out of the lavender button-down blouse and black pencil skirt. Donning a pair of leggings and an oversize Disturbing Tha Peace sweatshirt, she tucked her feet into a pair of bunny slippers and headed downstairs to make dinner.

She was at the stove, setting the oven to preheat, when Cooper bopped in, his white buds in his ears. She had no idea what he was listening to since he tended to silently mouth the lyrics rather than singing or rapping aloud. Walking toward her, he popped one bud out. "Are you cooking?"

"I was about to put in a pizza. I thought we'd have some salad on the side."

"It's cool, Ma. Ms. Bebe's gonna get us burgers on the way to the movie."

She reached into her waistband pocket. "Here's ten for your ticket."

He took the folded bill. "Thanks, Ma. I'm gonna go ahead over there." He gave her a dutiful hug and kiss on the cheek, popped his earbud back in and danced his way out the back door.

Ainsley put the pizza in the oven and dropped into a seat at the kitchen table. While the pizza cooked, she opened the budgeting app on her phone, adjusting for all the things Cooper had added to her plate today. The results were not good, and she could feel a frown creasing her face. *At this rate, I'll be selling one of my kidneys online.* It only served as another reminder that it was time for her to move up at work. She'd been executive assistant to Gage Woodson, chief operations officer at the fabled 404 Sound recording studio, for the last five and a half years. She knew the company like the back of her hand, and that's why she had her eye on a management position in human resources. If she could snag the job, it would come with her own office, parking spot and a sizable raise. The raise was the most enticing thing, based on her current situation.

I love my son—I swear I do. But the boy is costing me a mint!

She knew she was more than qualified for the position. But there was one problem: Gage. Her handsome yet incredibly closed-off boss. She'd been taking care of his demands for so long, she didn't know if anyone else could, or would, put up with him. Deep down, she felt a sense of loyalty to him, one that was likely tied to her raging crush on him. Yes, she'd been lusting after her boss pretty much since she'd accepted the position. So far, though, practicality and his tendency to stay locked in his office had kept her from acting on her feelings. How would he feel about her leaving her job as his assistant? Knowing Gage, he'd be annoyed at her for the inconvenience of having to replace her. Still, her dedication to Cooper trumped everything. If she got the job, she'd take it…and Gage would just have to figure it out.

Gage Woodson stifled a yawn as he flipped on the lights in his home gym at promptly six fifteen Saturday morning. While he did his best to stick to his workout routine, he didn't know if he'd ever think of himself as a morning person. Dressed in gray sweats and neon-green sneakers, he headed straight for the elliptical machine. Putting in his headphones and turning on his workout mix, he started pedaling.

He'd been on the machine about ten minutes when his baby brother, Miles, strolled in. Dressed in a black-and-white-striped tracksuit, he was sipping green juice from a plastic cup through a straw. "Morning, bro."

"Late as always," Gage quipped, raising the difficulty level on the machine just until the point his thigh muscles started to feel it. Keeping up with the pace of the classic Goodie Mob song in his ears helped him make the most of his workout. "What the hell are you drinking?"

Miles chuckled. "Power smoothie with liquid aminos. Gotta make it count, you know?" He climbed onto the recumbent bike next to him and started it up.

After thirty minutes, the two of them switched machines. Gage pedaled the bike a bit slower than the elliptical now that his thighs were protesting in earnest. Once they'd completed an hour of cardio, they headed to the weights.

Gage lay on his back on the bench while Miles set the weights on the bar. "You sure you can press 250, bro? That's your body weight plus like fifty mo'."

Gage rolled his eyes at his brother's teasing. "Just

set me up, Miles. Not everybody's arms are weak and spindly like yours."

Miles shook his head but did as he asked. As Gage lifted, Miles spotted him, and after twenty reps, Gage set the bar back in the bracket. "Any further questions?"

"Nah, you made your point." Miles traded positions with him. "But I'm not like you. So you can go ahead and bust that weight down to 180. I know my limits."

After they finished working out, the two brothers sat on Gage's screened back porch, protein shakes in hand. Mopping the sweat from his brow, Gage took a long drink from his shake. "Who wrote up the preliminary report on quarterly spending?"

"My lead accountant. You know, Kali Ramirez." Miles looked his way. "I signed off on it, though. Why do you ask?"

"I just can't get over that ten-thousand-dollar loss we took based on my actions."

Miles rolled his eyes. "Nobody blames you for that. At least, nobody in finance." As a chief financial officer, Miles managed the budget for the entire company. "It's not your fault, man."

"Yes, it is. I was stupid." He'd never forgive himself for trusting his ex-girlfriend the way he had and still felt responsible for replacing the funds she'd embezzled. "Why'd you list the loss as discretionary?"

"Kali did that. I approved it because it didn't fall into a cut-and-dried category like accounts payable or receivable." Miles waved him off. "We're just splitting hairs here, Gage. It's all semantics."

"I know, but…"

"Nah, bro. No buts. It's Saturday. Can you just stop talking about work for like five minutes?"

Gage cringed. "Sorry."

"I know it's not your fault you're so uptight. I guess you get it from Dad. But the least you can do is try not to give in to it. It's the weekend, nice weather and everything, and your ass is wound up tighter than the security lines at Hartsfield–Jackson."

As much as he hated to admit it, his brother was right. He'd always had a hard time disconnecting from work. His job as chief operations officer came with a high level of responsibility to his family, his employees and the shareholders, and he didn't take that lightly.

"Listen, though. I got a Tinder tale for you."

Gage shook his head. "Don't tell me you put your profile back up. I thought you said all you get are gold diggers?"

"That was before. This time I put up a picture in silhouette and gave a very vague description of my-self and my work." Miles rubbed his hands together. "I had six hits in two hours. Went out with this fine, thick shawty last night."

Gage listened to his brother spin a story about drinking at a bar before heading to one of the down-town Atlanta hotels with his "thick shawty," but his mind kept wandering back to work. Or more specifically, back to his gorgeous and extremely efficient executive assistant, Ainsley Voss. She had a body built for pleasure, a beautifully symmetrical face and silky dark hair. Yet, in the five-plus years he'd worked with her, he'd never approached her that way. She was just too good at her job, and he couldn't risk ruining it by asking her out on a date. His embezzling ex had also been a 404 Sound employee, and in the three years they'd dated, he told himself it was fine since she worked in another department. Well, that had blown up in his face in a spectacular way, and now, he was simply too skittish to make that mistake again.

Still, that didn't stop him from fantasizing about Ainsley. She kept her hair up in a bun on top of her head most of the time, with a sharp-line bang straight across her forehead, grazing her perfectly arched brows. In his fantasies, he'd undo that bun and let the dark riches of her hair fall around her shoulders. He'd run his fingers through it, inhaling the scent of fresh flowers that always seemed to follow her. Then he'd graze his fingertips along the hem of that fitted pencil skirt and...

"Gage!" Miles snapped his fingers. "Did you hear what I said, man?"

He shook his head, reluctantly returning to reality. "No, sorry. What?"

"I said, she had triple Ds, bro. *Triple. Ds.*" He made a juggling motion with his hands.

Gage laughed. "Miles, you're a hot-ass mess. And

what happens now that you've met her and she knows who you are?"

He shrugged. "I don't know. I'll probably see her again, just based on the strength of that rack." He laughed. "Nah, I'm kidding. She seems like a sweet girl, and I'll text her in a few days to see if she wants to get together again."

Shaking his head at his brother's antics, Gage finished off his shake and set the cup on the wicker coffee table in front of him. He remembered the requisition forms he'd left on the corner of his desk and cursed under his breath.

Miles frowned. "What's wrong with you?"

Knowing how his brother would react if he brought up work again, he shrugged it off. "Nothing. Just remembered something, but it can wait."

"Cool. Listen, you wanna hit up that pancake place for breakfast?"

"Yeah, we can do that." They did this almost every weekend—work out, then pig out. "But first I'm about to hit up the shower. Can't be going out all sweaty."

"Of course not. Ain't no Woodson man ever going out like that." Miles stood, stretching. "I'll use the downstairs while you use your master, then we'll change and head out."

Gage followed his brother back inside. "Sounds like a plan."

Two

When Ainsley walked into the 404 operations suite late Monday morning, she was met with the usual subdued silence. The suite, which occupied the eastern half of the second floor, contained Gage's office, the offices of two other operations staffers, a small conference room and a lobby area.

The lobby area featured soft gray walls and framed black-and-white photographs of artists who'd recorded at 404. One accent wall, painted a deep shade of red, held a framed poster-size photo of company owner Caleb Woodson with Todd "Speech" Thomas, lead vocalist and producer for the legendary Afrocentric hip-hop group Arrested Development.

Moving to her desk in the center of the lobby area,

she tucked her purse into the top drawer. With her company tablet and stylus in hand, she walked down the corridor, past the three closed office doors, to the conference room at the end.

As usual, she was the first to arrive for the department's monthly meeting. Inside the empty conference room, she flipped the switch, flooding the room with soft LED lighting. The polished black lacquer table, with six matching upholstered chairs pulled up to it, showed a reflection of the chandelier above.

Opening the blinds, she set up a pitcher of water and glasses in the center of the table, then took her seat to the right of the seat at the head. While waiting for the others, she used her tablet to peruse the *Greater Fulton Business Journal*'s article on Shana Dresden. After more than twenty years as 404's manager of human resources, Mrs. Dresden would retire in early spring. *And with any luck, I'll be the one to fill her position. I spent the start of my career in HR and I know this company like the back of my hand—I'm perfect for this job.*

Production manager Kelly Ross was first to arrive, with marketing manager Duval Anderson close behind her. After the two management staffers took their seats, the three of them exchanged morning pleasantries while Ainsley closed the article and opened her notes app in anticipation of Gage's arrival.

He strode in a few minutes later, commanding her attention as he did every time he entered a room.

He wore a charcoal-gray suit, bright red shirt and a black-and-gray-striped tie. His tall crown of curls and full beard were impeccably groomed, and as he set his tablet down on the table, his arresting brown eyes swept over the room. "Good morning, all." As his gaze met hers, it lingered for a few long moments.

She swallowed. *Why does he have to be so fine?* While her insides melted, outwardly she offered a small smile and nod of greeting.

His answering smile only melted her further.

He took his seat, then clapped his hands together. "Let's get started, shall we? Duval, what's happening in marketing?"

Duval cleared his throat and ran a hand over his close-trimmed fade. "We're testing a new layout for the website to improve ease of use. We also updated the forms for artists and managers to book private studio tours or for them to book studio time."

"Great. And what did you come up with for artist outreach?" Gage leaned forward in his seat.

"I'm running ads on SoundCloud, with several versions to test for efficacy. The purpose is to show artists the benefits of recording with us."

While they talked, Ainsley used her stylus to jot down notes on what was said.

"Sounds good. Kelly, what can you report on the production front?"

Kelly pulled out a pencil she'd tucked into her reddish-brown curls and began tapping the small yellow legal pad as she rattled off the information.

"We had four albums produced at 404 in January. Of the four, one went over the predetermined recording time and that artist paid for an additional twenty hours of billable time."

Gage's smile brightened. "Sucks for them, but I'm sure that padded the bottom line nicely. What about this month?"

"We're on track for five albums this month, with a total of 370 projected billable hours…assuming all goes well with the new sound equipment for Studio 1A."

Gage scratched his chin, and once again, his gaze swung toward her. "Ainsley, do we have a status update on the equipment?"

Switching apps on her tablet, Ainsley ran a check on the tracking number for the shipment. Her brow furrowed as the results appeared. *Oh shit.* "It says… shipment lost."

Gage's eyes flashed. "What?" She was sure he'd heard her the first time; he just hadn't liked the answer.

"It says, 'shipment lost.'"

Kelly whistled. Duval cringed.

Gage sighed aloud. "We don't have time for this. We need the studio ready when Organized Noize brings in The Visionary." He ran a hand over his face. "It's been, what, ten years since they debuted a new artist? We can't lose this contract."

She scrolled down, looking for the contact information. "I'll get to the bottom of it. I'm calling the shipper's customer service line."

"Thank you. In the meantime, the meeting's dismissed." Gage stood. "Try to keep everything else running while we deal with this equipment mess."

After Kelly and Duval packed up and left, Ainsley called the shipper's eight-hundred number and waited on hold. While she drummed her fingertips on the tabletop, her boss watched her with an intense, expectant gaze. She could feel the tension rolling off him like a heavy fog over a lake. There wasn't anything she could do but wait for the moment, and under his scrutiny, the waiting seemed to drag on forever. She purposely leaned back in her chair and kept her gaze fixed on the ceiling, knowing that if she looked at him, she'd find only those intoxicating brown eyes. Hell, she couldn't even hazard a glance at the table because the surface was far too reflective.

Finally, a voice came on the line. "How can I help you?"

Ainsley immediately gave her name, stated her problem and rattled off the tracking number for the studio equipment. After a few moments of listening to the rep's typing in the background, she confirmed that the crates holding the equipment were indeed lost. "How? And what is your company planning to do to locate our items or to remedy this?"

The rep rattled off a scripted dialogue about an account credit for future shipping and advised her that a refund for the items would be processed in six to eight weeks after some paperwork. Hanging up, she looked to Gage. "I'm sorry, Gage. It looks like the equipment is legit lost."

"Well, fuck." Gage ran a hand over his face. "I can't let this happen. I've got to get in contact with Marshall Harcroft, now." He came around to her seat, leaning over her shoulder. "Pull up the number, please."

As he moved closer to her, the spicy scent of his Dior cologne invaded her nostrils. The heat of his nearness washed over her, raising her body temperature so much that she could feel the beads of sweat forming around her hairline. He smelled heavenly, and she could feel her brain turning to mush. *Nothing turns me on like a well-groomed, good-smelling man. How am I supposed to focus on work with him this close?*

She did as he asked, immediately locating the number for Harcroft Sound Limited. "Do you want me to call?"

He shook his head, leaning over her shoulder to see the number on her tablet. "I'll do it."

His forearm brushed her shoulder, and she saw stars. Swallowing hard, she said. "Okay, whatever you think is best."

He'd already dialed the number and had his phone against his ear. "Come into my office, Ainsley. We need to talk."

Gage ceased his pacing when Ainsley entered his office. He allowed himself a brief perusal of her beauty. The sunlight flowing through his office window cast an almost ethereal glow on her golden skin. She wore a navy pencil skirt, yellow button-down blouse and yellow pumps. Her hair was on top of her head in that tight little bun she favored, and gold hoops sparkled in her lobes. His eyes connected with hers, and the sparkle he saw there threatened to stop his heart. *Why must she be so stunning?*

"I'm guessing you're still on hold."

He swallowed, trying to focus on her words and not the glossy lips they'd passed through. "I am. I just don't understand how they could have lost such a valuable shipment."

She shrugged. "Who knows? But it doesn't look like we'll get much help from the shipper, so Harcroft is our best hope." She pushed an errant curl away from her face.

He rubbed his hand over his eyes. "Good thinking. Once someone actually picks up, I'll find out everything I can." Harcroft Sound Limited, a boutique company located in San Leandro, California, made all the soundboards and equipment used in 404's studios. Harcroft engineers built each system by hand, directly to the specifications of the person who placed the order. Their skilled craftsmanship of the equipment was what gave 404 the unique, high-quality sound people had come to associate with the company. "The equipment in Studio 1 is dying fast. After twenty years in service, we can't really be mad about it. But the last thing I need right now is a mishap."

"Agreed." She shifted her weight from side to side, clutching her trusty tablet in the crook of her arm. "Is there anything else you need from me right now?"

He gestured to his guest chair. "Have a seat. When they come on the line, I'll put them on speaker, and you make a note of everything they say."

"Yes, sir." She sat, crossing her legs demurely, the tablet resting on her knee.

He pressed the speakerphone button, filling the room with the sounds of the hold music. It was a track by Herb Alpert & the Tijuana Brass, a sultry Latin tune. Looking across the desk at Ainsley, who busied herself by twirling her stylus like a tiny baton between her fingers, he couldn't help thinking how the music matched his perceptions of her. She was beautiful, inviting, smooth and silky with a little kick.

She glanced up at him then, as if suddenly aware of his attention.

Their gazes locked for a moment.

Her lips puckered, slowly, almost imperceptibly.

He swallowed. *Are those lips as soft as they look?* Heaven help him, he wanted to know. And there was only one way to find out. He eased to the edge of his chair, leaning forward.

The music stopped, and a female voice announced, "Harcroft Sound Limited, how can I help you?"

Clearing his throat, Gage sat back in his chair.

"Good morning. This is Gage Woodson at 404 Sound out of Atlanta. I need to speak with Marshall."

"Mr. Harcroft has a full day of meetings, and…"

He tamped down his frustration, knowing the receptionist didn't deserve to bear the brunt of it. "Listen, I don't want to sound rude. But I know Marshall is at his desk every morning by seven. We're missing a large, expensive order. And since 404 spends hundreds of thousands of dollars with your company, I'm going to need you to get Mr. Harcroft on the phone."

"Give me just a moment, Mr. Woodson."

"Thank you." He sighed as the hold music returned, though this time it was a jazz composition featuring Ella and Louis on vocals.

"At least their hold music isn't too bad," Ainsley remarked with a half smirk. "Place I called last week had me listening to an acoustic version of a Snoop Doggy Dogg song."

"Yikes." Despite himself, he felt a smile tug his lips. That's how she was. Even in the most stressful of situations, she always seemed to know when to infuse a little humor in the situation.

"Hello, Gage?"

"Marshall, good morning. Ainsley is here with me, too." Gage tented his fingers, turning his attention back to the matter at hand. "I'm calling because our equipment seems to have gone missing."

"I'm sorry to hear that, Gage. Any details from the shipper?"

"Not many," Ainsley volunteered. "There was

some sort of malfunction with the tracking system, and the equipment went off the radar somewhere between Oakland and Vegas."

"Sheesh." Marshall's tone conveyed a mixture of frustration and embarrassment. "I'd give it until the end of the day, just to see if it turns up, either at your door or in their tracking system."

"Fair enough, but what if it doesn't appear by then?" Gage could feel the knot of tension tightening the area between his shoulder blades.

"Unfortunately, you'll have to reorder. At no additional cost, of course."

Gage cringed. "That's good to know, Marshall. But the money's not the issue here so much as time." That wasn't entirely true, especially not if Miles were consulted. Gage knew his number-crunching, budget-minded younger brother would freak if they had to dip into the company coffers to pay for another custom-built studio set. "I know that what you all do at Harcroft is a very delicate operation."

"You're right. If need be, we can put a rush on the order. You know, have a few extra hands working on it." Marshall sighed. "Let's hope it doesn't come to that."

Gage ran a hand over his face. "Okay. Thanks for your help, Marshall."

"No problem. Let me know by 5:00 p.m. Pacific Time if you need to reorder."

After ending the call, he looked over at Ainsley,

who'd been busily jotting on the tablet. "Did you get all that?"

She nodded. "I did."

He blew out a breath. "Thanks. Keep an eye on the tracking throughout the day. If you don't have any updates by four thirty, let me know so I can get Marshall and his crew back on the job."

"Yes, sir." She tucked her stylus behind her ear. "Anything else?"

He scratched his chin, watching her. For some reason, he didn't want her to return to her desk just yet. His mind ran through a series of tasks he could give her to keep her in the office with him. Looking into those rich, honey-brown eyes, he found it harder and harder to concentrate. *This is why I avoid working alone with her as much as possible. She's the most pleasant distraction I've ever had to overcome.* Finally, he shook his head. "No. You're free to go."

She stood then. "I'll be at my desk if you need me." Turning away, she strolled out of the office, taking the sweet, floral aroma of her presence with her. The moment she was gone, the office felt somewhat empty.

What was it about Ainsley Voss that seemed to be his undoing? He considered himself a man of poise and control. Yet, whenever she entered his personal space, he felt like a young boy fawning over his first crush. After more than five years of working with her, of trying to deny or avoid the way she made

him feel, his fascination with her remained just as
strong as ever.

If his hunch was right, she had feelings for him as
well. But he knew better than to approach her. The
dynamic that existed between them as boss and employee meant that coming on to her was out of the
question. His foolish heart had already led him to
one workplace disaster, and he didn't need another.
Beyond that, he'd never want to make Ainsley uncomfortable.

*No, if things move forward between us, it has to
be on her terms.*

Ainsley returned to her desk and sat down. Drawing a deep breath, she cracked her knuckles and
nudged her mouse to awaken the computer from its
slumber. *If this shipment really is lost, Gage is going
to panic, big-time.*

Everyone in operations knew how much was riding on the safe and timely arrival of the new studio
equipment, and no one bore more responsibility for
that than her boss. Anticipating the coming storm,
she set about doing the work to prepare for it.

Grabbing her phone, she placed a quick call to
Mike, one of the interns who worked on their floor,
and asked him to run an errand for her around four
fifteen. That done, she opened her top drawer and
searched through her collection of essential oils for
the ones she needed. Locating the tiny vials, she

tucked them into a drawstring bag and set them on the corner of her desk.

She opened the folder titled "404-411" that she kept in her cloud, then opened her internet browser. Accessing the company server, she read the most recent company newsletter. Using her stylus, she highlighted items of importance as she read. When she finished with the newsletter, she pulled every single internal memo, regardless of department, that had been published during the last week. Each memo received the same read-and-highlight treatment as the newsletter.

She got up for a quick stretch and grabbed two bottles of water from the break-room fridge. Knowing Gage's tendency to forget to drink water when he got wrapped up in his work, she placed a bottle on the corner of his desk. He glanced up from his tablet, gave a nod of appreciation and grabbed the water. When she saw him unscrew the cap and take a long draw, she left, taking the other bottle back to her desk.

After reading all six memos, she dragged them, as well as the newsletter file, into her cloud folder. This was a weekly routine for her, something she'd done ever since she joined the company. It kept her informed on all the moving parts that made 404 tick. Tracking these things served a dual purpose for her: satisfying her curiosity about the inner workings of the company and making her more efficient at her job.

At twenty minutes past four, an email arrived in

her inbox from the shipping company. Opening it, she read it silently. She could feel her eyes widening as she read about the fate of their equipment. When she closed the email, she drew a deep, cleansing breath. Gathering the drawstring bag, her portable diffuser and her wits, she went to Gage's office to deliver the news.

She found him leaning back in his chair, reading something off his tablet. He looked up when she entered the room, setting the tablet aside. "Did we get word on the equipment?"

"Yes." Before saying anything else, she set the battery-powered diffuser on the corner of his desk. After adding a few drops of lavender and clary sage oils to the dispenser, she turned the device on, silently watching as the cool mist began to fill the air.

Gage looked at the diffuser, then up at her. "Oh no. You bringing that thing in here means it's bad news."

She swallowed. "I just got an email. According to the shipper, the equipment was stolen off a truck sometime after it left Cali. They just located it in Reno."

He cringed. "I'm gonna go out on a limb here and say it's not in usable condition anymore."

She shook her head. "Somebody smashed the crate and grabbed most of the components." She sighed. "Nothing left but a tangle of loose wires and some plastic housings."

He slammed his hand on the desk. "Damn." His

eyes flashed. "I don't believe this. After all these years of using that same equipment, we finally upgrade and this happens? Unbelievable."

"Gage, I know this is stressful." She leaned against the edge of the desk.

"Stressful is an understatement." He stood, started pacing the floor. "We've got five albums coming up this month. What the hell are the artists supposed to use? The old equipment just isn't going to produce the high-quality sound we're known for. Not anymore. It's obsolete. We can't just…"

"Okay, okay. I get it, you're upset. But this isn't productive." She placed a hand on his shoulder, trying to ignore the charge she got from feeling his muscle flex beneath her hand. Guiding him back to his seat, she gave a gentle nudge to get him to sit. "You know the drill. Take deep breaths."

He frowned. "Oh, come on. I don't…"

She tilted her head to the side, held his gaze so he would know she was serious. "Deep breaths, Gage."

He relented, settling back in his seat. He inhaled, slow and deep, then blew the breath out through his mouth, the way she'd trained him to do in situations like this.

She observed, watching the rise of his shoulders as he took in air and hearing the whoosh as he released the air through his full lips.

A knock at the office door drew her attention. Turning toward the door, she smiled. "Thanks, Mike. You're right on time." Walking toward the young intern, she took the clear plastic cup from his hand. After Mike left, she handed the chilled cup over to Gage.

He accepted it, his jaw visibly relaxing. "A peanut butter protein shake from the Powerhouse. When did you order this?"

"Hours ago. Just in case things went to the left."

A ghost of a smile came over his face as he took his first sip. "You know me too well, Ainsley."

She shrugged. "Just doing my job." There was more to it than that, but she had no plans to tell him how she felt. It would only complicate things between them if he knew she thought the world of him.

He set the cup down and sighed. "Looks like I'm reordering that equipment. And this time, it absolutely has to get here in one piece."

"I've been thinking about that." She sat in the chair opposite him. "And I've got an idea…"

Three

Tuesday morning, Ainsley fought her way through Atlanta traffic to make it to work on time. As she inched her way down I-20, her phone rang, the sound cutting through her music as it filled the car's cabin. Engaging her hands-free calling, she answered. "Hello?"

"Hey, coz. What's up?"

She smiled at the sound of Eden's voice. "Hey! You know what's up here. It's Atlanta at rush hour, and I-20 is a cross between a parking lot and a race-track."

Eden laughed. "Every hour is rush hour in the ATL. And I gotta say, I don't miss it."

"Must be nice getting chauffeured around New York, huh?"

"It is, I'm not gonna lie." She said something to someone in the background, the sound muffled. "I've mostly been at the studio with Chanel, though. Not too much sightseeing."

She sighed as she reached a stoplight just as it turned red. "What's it like working with Chanel the Titan?"

"Lots of late nights. Just coming off an all-nighter, actually." She yawned.

"So that explains why you're up so early. You never went to bed." Ainsley chuckled as she finally got within a few miles of 404's headquarters. "Make sure you get some rest."

"You don't have to tell me twice. As soon as I leave here, I'm going back to my hotel room and climbing straight into bed." She yawned again. "What's going on at work?"

Ainsley rolled her eyes. "Pandemonium. That big studio equipment order got lost during shipping."

"Oh shit."

"*Oh shit* is right. We waited until the end of the day yesterday to see if it would turn up in the shipper's system."

"They never found it?"

"That's just it. They did find it. Or what was left of it."

Eden whistled. "That doesn't sound good."

"You're telling me." She briefly recapped what had happened to their order.

"I'm gonna guess Gage didn't take the news well."

She shook her head, recalling yesterday's events. "He took it better than I'd expect, but I know he was freaking out on the inside. I suggested Gage fly out and personally escort the reordered equipment back to Atlanta, and he nearly chewed my head off. I'm not looking forward to what's gonna happen today." She thought back to the tight set of his jaw as he'd gone on and on about how he couldn't afford to be away from the office at a time like this when everything at 404 Sound was in flux. Still, she knew she'd given him a solid idea. It was up to him whether he took her advice or not.

"Whew. Hang in there, Ains. I'm sure he'll come around."

"If he wants Studio 1 up and running for that new artist, he doesn't have a choice."

"That reminds me. I saw a social media post about Shana in HR retiring. You should apply."

She hesitated. "I was thinking about it, but I haven't made up my mind…"

"Ainsley." Eden's stern tone almost sounded like her mother's. "You worked in HR in two different companies for years before working for Gage. Do it. You know 404 Sound likes to hire from within, and who knows how things work around there better than you? No one. Get on it today."

"Hold on, don't jump down my throat. There's

still plenty of time. I just need to tweak my résumé a bit, and then I'm on it."

"Okay. But make sure you get it done before the week is out. We both know you're ready to move up into management. Gage will probably be lost without you, but that's his problem."

Ainsley agreed. "You're right. And don't worry, I'll take care of that application."

"Good. Well, enough work talk. How's Coop?"

"He's doing fine. My pockets are crying, though." She shook her head, thinking of all the recent expenses he'd brought to her attention. "I feel like he's got me by the ankles, shaking me for spare change at this point."

"I sent you a little something."

She sighed. "Eden, you don't have to do that."

"I know I don't. But I want to. Remember what I said when Cooper needed that surgery?"

"Yeah, I remember. You said we're in this together."

"Right. And that hasn't changed just because I'm in New York." She paused. "So, no more arguments because it's already done." A notification from her Money Pop app sounded, and she fought back the tears welling in her eyes. "I love you, Eden."

"Love you, too, Ains. I'll talk to you later."

Focusing back on the road, Ainsley stopped off at the Bodacious Bean to grab Gage's morning coffee. She picked up this same order every morning, so when she walked in, the barista handed her the order before could even finish saying *good morning*. Leaving a tip in the fishbowl on the counter, she returned to her car.

When she arrived at the office, she knocked on his closed door. Moments later, he swung it open.

Gage Woodson. Mr. Take Charge. Groomed from his youth to step into leadership at the company, and that preparation was always on display. From his tailored suits to his commanding presence, everything about him fairly screamed, "I run this."

Today's charcoal suit, paired with a royal blue shirt and silver tie, was no exception. His lips tilted into a slight smile. "Good morning, Ainsley."

"Good morning." She handed over the coffee and the paper bag holding his Tuesday pastry—a slice of banana bread. With a nod, she turned and started to walk away.

"Hold on."

At the sound of his request, she stopped and faced him again. "Yes?"

"I…just wanted to apologize for the way I acted yesterday afternoon." He rested his shoulder against the door frame, placing one hand over his chest.

Her brow hitched. *I don't know if I ever heard him apologize before.* Still, he looked pretty contrite at the moment. "Okay."

"What I did yesterday wasn't okay. I snapped at you because I was under a lot of stress about the equipment, but that's no excuse."

She nodded slowly. "I understand. And consider it water under the bridge."

"I appreciate that." He cleared his throat. "Also, I wanted to let you know that I'm going to take your advice. If I weren't in such a funk yesterday, I would have taken it then."

She swallowed. "I…um… I'm glad you found my suggestion helpful."

"I did. I just wish I'd been able to see it sooner." His gaze intensified. "You're an invaluable asset to this company, Ainsley. And to me."

She felt her heart pounding in her ears. "Thank you."

"No, thank you." He reached for her hand, gave it a squeeze. "I'm meeting with my mother and sister at lunch today, and we're going to discuss the best way to put your brilliant plan in motion."

"Sounds good. Do you need me to attend?"

He shook his head. "No. I'll fill you in on all the details when I get back." He paused, his gaze dropping slightly.

She squirmed inwardly. *If I didn't know better, I'd say he was staring at my lips.* She could feel that familiar heat building inside, the same heat she felt whenever they occupied the same space for too long. "Great. So…if you don't need anything else, I'm just gonna head over to my desk."

Their eyes met again, and she thought she saw a twinkle of mischief. He released her hand, though he seemed somewhat reluctant to do so. "You're good to go. I just wanted to thank you."

As she turned and walked away, she could feel his gaze on her back. Determined not to let him see her sweat, she headed down the corridor and back to her desk as fast as her pumps would carry her.

Seated, she booted up her computer in an attempt at productivity. But in the back of her mind, the question loomed larger than anything else.

Was Gage Woodson flirting with me? After all these years, he's chosen now *to flirt? Just when I'm about to apply for the HR position? Did I make a wrong turn and walk into the damn Twilight Zone or what?*

Sitting in the homey, familiar atmosphere of Mary Mac's Tea Room, Gage perused the menu. The place was an institution, a jewel of downtown Atlanta since 1945. Once, there'd been a total of sixteen similar establishments in the city. Today, only Mary Mac's remained, as both a nostalgic reminder of the genteel glamour of early-twentieth-century Atlanta and a respite from the fast-paced, tech-driven world outside its doors. He'd eaten here more times than he could count over the years, and the food and service never disappointed. *My only real worry is that I'll eat so well, I'll be too sleepy to go on with the rest of the workday.*

"This is my favorite place to come for lunch," Addison remarked from her seat next to him. "It's such a nice escape from whatever's going on at the office."

"True indeed, Mama." Nia, seated across from them, flipped her menu over to look at the desserts. "Besides, getting in here around dinnertime is damn near impossible."

He chuckled. Most ATLiens knew that if they were craving Mary Mac's delicacies after work, they had better be prepared for a long wait. "How are things on the third floor, Mom?"

Addison shrugged. "Fine, for the most part." Her role as company vice president was largely ceremonial, yet his sister Nia always consulted their parents on any major business decision, out of an abundance of love and respect.

His brow cocked because something in her tone gave him pause. "Something bothering you?"

"I just know it's time for me to start planning our thirtieth-anniversary celebration, and part of me is dreading all the work it's going to take." She released a small sigh.

"It's such an exciting milestone to reach. It's still a few months away. You know you have all of us to help you if it gets to be too much." Nia sipped from her glass of sweet tea. "This is a family business, so planning the celebration will be a family affair."

Addison's expression softened a bit in response to her daughter's declaration. "Thanks for the reminder, Nia."

The server came to take their orders. Nia ordered

smothered chicken and a side of turnip greens. Addison got a baked sweet potato with okra and tomatoes, as well as spiced apples.

Mom's still vegan, I see. He had no such aspirations to cut meat from his diet. Since this was his once-weekly cheat meal, he asked for the half slab of barbecued ribs with a side of mac and cheese.

After the server left, Gage rested his forearms on the table, lacing his fingers together. "So, I'm gonna guess you already heard about what happened to our new studio equipment?"

Nia blew out a breath. "We have. I got an inter-office memo from Miles."

"What a mess. And what in the world are those people intending to do with the parts?" Addison shook her head.

"Who knows?" He couldn't imagine another use for the parts. "It doesn't really matter what they plan on doing with them. We're just going to have to replace that equipment, and the sooner, the better."

"Right." Nia's face morphed into that serious expression she always wore when she was thinking about business matters. She tilted her head slightly to the right, sucking in her bottom lip. "I can't say I have any faith in that shipping company. Frankly, their security and tracking are terrible."

"We never should have switched shippers," Gage admitted, his eyes on the white tablecloth. "That's on me. I wanted to give a small shipping outfit a chance with us and save a little money on shipping costs while I was at it." That had backfired, big-time.

Addison waved him off. "There was no way you could have anticipated a mess like this. Don't worry about it."

Oh, I'm plenty worried about it. But he saw no need to verbalize that. "As I see it, we're just going to have to make sure the reordered equipment makes it here, intact and on time."

His sister nodded. "I agree. So, what's the plan? Are we going back to our old reliable shipping company?"

He shook his head. "Even better. I'm going to pick up the equipment myself, in person."

Their plates came, and as they each dug into the delectable offerings, conversation at the table ceased, replaced by the clinking sound of their silverware striking the china plates.

Gage quipped, "Ever notice how quiet it gets when Black people are eating?"

Nia giggled. "Only if the food is good."

With a shake of her head, their mother asked, "Now, what were you saying about picking up the equipment, Gage?" She forked up a bit of sweet potato.

"Oh yeah. I'm just going to go and get it myself. The only way I can be sure it gets here is to personally escort it."

Nia chewed a piece of chicken, her expression

thoughtful. "Makes sense to me. It's a long haul to California, though."

"I know. Besides that, I'll need room for the equipment." Gage swiped a napkin over his mouth. "That's why I was going to ask for use of the company jet."

"I don't think it will be a problem."

"Great." Gage leaned back in his chair.

Another period of quiet descended as they enjoyed their lunch.

"Max is back from vacation." Addison polished off her spiced apples. "I'm sure she's ready to get back in the air."

Gage nodded. Maxine Kidder had been the company pilot for the last ten years and was as professional as they came. Flying with her was always a pleasure. "Sounds good."

"When do you want to fly out?" Nia posed the question as she finished off her greens.

"Monday. That's when Marshall promised the new order will be ready." He pushed away his empty plate. "The plan is to fly out Monday morning and be back in town that night. If all goes well, everything will be installed, up and running by Wednesday."

"And when was The Visionary supposed to start using his studio time?" Nia ran a hand over her short curls, then raised it for the check.

"The following Monday. We're cutting it a lot closer than I would prefer, but it is what it is." *The situation isn't ideal, but I figure we're good as long as we can get Studio 1 back in working shape before our artist shows up to record.* "I'm not about to miss out on this. Having Organized Noize in our studio is a hell of a big deal."

"Absolutely." Nia accepted the check from the server and flipped the leather folder open. "It's not just the revenue, it's the notoriety that comes from working with such a legendary production team." After placing her credit card in the folder, she said, "Just have Ainsley fill out the electronic requisition, and I'll have Ariel reach out to Max to get everything organized."

"Okay." Hearing Ainsley's name brought a vision of her into his head. She was the picture of beauty and poise, always carrying that tablet and stylus, always listening and taking notes. Still, her particular brand of witty commentary was a bright spot in his day and had kept him alert during many a dull meeting. And lately he noticed the aroma that followed her, hanging around her like a cloud. He couldn't for the life of him figure out what it was—maybe a new perfume, or lotion, or whatever hair products she used to make her curls shine. The scent was an intoxicating blend of florals, and he found himself inhaling deeply whenever she left the room, just so he could enjoy the remnants that lingered in her wake.

"It was a great idea to go get the equipment in person, son." Addison smiled at him.

"Thanks, Mom." He thought about Ainsley and how she'd been the one to mention that. But he'd already thanked her and saw no need to make the conversation awkward by bringing that up. But he did have another idea, one that would benefit them both.

Ainsley should come with me to California.

On her way back from her lunch break, Ainsley took the elevator down to the basement. Once there, she pushed through the glass doors into the company mailroom, heading straight for the pickup desk.

Mallory Evans, head mail clerk, looked up and smiled as she approached. "Hey, Ainsley. How are you?"

"We've had a little drama in operations, but I can't complain." Picking up a pen from the cup on the desk, she signed the logbook in the proper place.

Mallory whistled. "Oh, I've heard. The CEO's secretary was in here right before lunch. What a shame about the equipment, but at least your boss is going to use the company jet to retrieve the new set himself." She shuffled through the files on her desk, pulling out the familiar blue folder. "Here's the letters for your department. Hang tight for a minute. I've got a couple of boxes in the back for you."

Ainsley watched with a smile as Mallory quickly crossed the mailroom. She knew she would hear the latest info on company happenings whenever she stopped by the mailroom, and Mallory's info had proven valuable to her on more than one occasion. Today's tidbit served as proof that Gage had taken her advice and would be picking up the new sound equipment in person.

After getting the rest of the mail, she returned to the office on the third floor. When she walked in, she was surprised to find Gage standing by her desk. "Hi, Gage. Do you need something?"

He turned her way, his dark eyes connecting with hers. "Yes, actually. I wanted to let you know I'm making arrangements to go to California."

"So you're putting my idea in motion, then?"

"I am. I told you I would. Why wouldn't I? It's a great idea." He paused. "I also wanted to ask you if you'd consider coming with me."

She stopped short, one of the packages falling out of her hands and hitting the floor with a thump. "Really?"

"Yes." He walked over, retrieving the fallen item. "I think the whole process will go much smoother if you're there with me."

She swallowed. Her heart fluttered at the idea of being in the close confines of the company jet with her handsome boss. Yet the logical side of her wouldn't allow her too much excitement. Would she be able to keep herself from doing or saying anything that would make things awkward between them? Something that would alter their relationship forever, something she couldn't take back?

"Ainsley?"

Aware of his scrutiny, she stammered a reply. "I... yes, I guess."

His brow hitched. "I need to know if you're going so I can tell Max to prepare for two passengers."

"When?"

"Monday." He read the label on the package he'd picked up, then tucked it beneath his arm. "This whole situation with the first order has put us off schedule, so I need to get the equipment here as quickly as possible. We need Studio 1 up and running."

She drew a deep breath, moving to her desk to put the mail down. "How long would we be gone?"

"Only a day. My plan is to fly there, do the paperwork, secure the equipment and fly back that same day."

She paused for a moment. "I just need to ask Bebe to look after Cooper when he gets out of school, then. As long as she can do that, I should be able to go."

He smiled. "Great. Can you let me know for sure by the end of the day?"

She nodded. "Just let me text Bebe."

His smile broadened. "Sounds good. I'm really looking forward to this." He gestured at the pile of mail she'd brought in. "Is any of the rest of that mine?"

She flipped through the stack of envelopes and handed three of them to him. "Just these."

"Thanks, Ainsley. You're the best." With a wink, he disappeared around the corner into the corridor.

Is it just me, or is he being overly charming?

She flopped into her chair and willed her pulse

to slow. There was something about him, something she'd been aware of since her first day on the job but still couldn't quite name. The longer she looked into his eyes, the more it affected her...whatever it was.

She sent a quick text to Bebe. Leaning against her backrest, she took a moment to think about their conversation. Did he really need her along to help with the business of getting the equipment back to the studio? Or did he just want to spend time with her?

She'd been on company trips before on the jet, with Gage, other members of the executive team and their respective assistants. This would be the first time she traveled alone with him. He'd always been a gentleman, so she had no worries about his behavior. It was her own possible actions that had her concerned.

None of this was of any consequence now. After all, she'd basically agreed to go with him.

Bebe's reply came—she had no problem watching Cooper for a few hours after school.

Dismissing the message, Ainsley drew another deep breath and went to Gage's office to let him know that she would be traveling with him.

Four

Thursday afternoon, Ainsley was back in Gage's office, jotting down notes on her tablet as he rattled off instructions for their upcoming trip to California. *I wasn't really surprised when he asked me to come along.* It had been ages since she'd been on a vacation, and she wasn't one to turn down a free cross-country flight, on a private jet no less.

At the moment, he was on the phone with Max, the longtime company pilot, chatting about the flight. "Well, Max, I'm glad to hear your schedule's clear next week. We'll only need you for Monday, though. How does a quick run to Cali and back sound?"

The sound of Max's laugh came over the speaker-phone before she spoke. "I wouldn't call it a quick run, Gage. It's a little over four hours each way. But it sounds great."

"Excellent. Once we make it to Harcroft and properly pack up our equipment, we can head home. I see no reason we won't be back by that night."

"I got you. What time do you want to push off?"

His eyes shifted to her. "Ainsley, can you be ready to leave by eight thirty?"

She nodded. "That's fine." *Cooper's bus leaves at 7:10 a.m.*

"Can we say eight thirty for takeoff?" Gage asked.

Max replied, "I'll put it in my logbook. Anything else?"

"No."

"Cool. See you Monday." Max disconnected the call. "Great. Now, with that set up—" he turned his gaze on her "—I'll need you to make sure the plane is stocked with these items."

She nodded, taking down his words. The list mostly consisted of his protein shakes, muscle-building snack bars, fresh fruit and bottles of spring water. *He's all about maintaining his physique. Can't say I blame him.* Dragging her gaze over his body, she thought it was definitely something worth preserving.

"I'm just going to double-check with Marshall at Harcroft." He picked up his desk phone and dialed the number. "Before we get too deep into trip planning, I need to make sure the reorder will actually be ready in time."

She waited while he had a brief conversation with Marshall. All the while she tried not to imagine him working out. The struggle was all too real. In her mind's eye, she could see him running on a treadmill, shirtless, with rivulets of sweat running down his muscled back...

"Ainsley?"

His voice calling her name snapped her back to reality. "I'm sorry, what was that?"

"I asked how old your son is now. Will he be okay on his own on Monday?"

She cleared her throat, a bit taken aback by his question. Gage seldom asked about her child. "Oh. Yes. Cooper's eleven. My neighbor will watch him until I get home."

He nodded. "What's that like? Having an eleven-year-old? I don't have much experience with kids."

She shrugged. "It's an adventure. He's old enough to do a lot for himself but young enough to still be needy at times."

He leaned forward. "For example?"

"He has a key to the house, but he forgets it at least once a week. That sort of thing."

"I see." He chuckled. "Well, my hat's off to you. I don't know how parents do it. Just seems like an awful lot of work to not get paid for."

He's not wrong. Parenting involved a lot of unpaid labor. Still, something about the way he said it just...didn't sit right. "Thanks... I guess."

"Trust me, it's a compliment. I mean, my siblings

still manage to get on our parents' nerves, and we're all grown." He shook his head. "I guess it's unpaid work you never get to retire from."

"Speaking of children, you know those kids from Keystone Middle are touring the building today, right?" She watched him, gauging his reaction.

He swallowed. "Damn, is that today?"

She nodded. "It was on the calendar. I sent you a reminder a week ago. And yesterday. And this morning." *Does he bother to check the notifications I send to his phone?*

"I forgot. I've been so wrapped up in the equipment drama I hadn't even thought about it." He ran a hand over his dark curls. "I don't have to make a speech or anything, do I?"

"No. The kids will only be here for an hour or two, touring the building and seeing how things work at a recording studio, both in the booth and in the offices." She'd been looking forward to the school visit. She loved kids, and their presence would be a nice change of pace to the sometimes stale, too-serious vibe of the office. "They'll only swing by here briefly."

"I hope we'll get a warning before they show up." Gage stood, straightening the lapels of his sport coat. "I want a little heads-up before they come up here destroying anything."

She frowned, aware of the dismissiveness in his tone. *What's his problem?* Yes, they were children, but these were older kids. Middle schoolers, so around Cooper's age. They tended to be much more mature and far less accident-prone than their younger counterparts. "I'll let Kim at the front desk know to give me a call when the students are on their way upstairs. Do you need anything else from me at the moment?"

He shook his head. "No. You can go on back to your desk." He gave her a crooked half smile. "Just warn me before the youngsters descend on us, okay?"

"I will." She stood, taking her tablet and stylus with her down the short corridor and back to her desk.

She was in the thick of her work when she got a call around three that the students from Keystone were on their way up. She knocked softly on Gage's door, and when he opened it, she met him with a smile. "The kids are coming."

He took a deep breath, checked his watch. "Okay. I can only spare a few minutes before I have to leave to meet my dad for dinner. With traffic being what it is, I need to get outta here by four."

Wondering why her boss looked so nervous at the prospect of entertaining a few twelve-year-olds, she walked to the suite door and waited.

They arrived a few minutes later, a group of about ten middle-schoolers and their accompanying adult. According to the interoffice memo, the students were members of Keystone's entrepreneurship club. Opening the door, she welcomed them and their chaperone inside. "I'm Ainsley Voss. Welcome to 404 Sound."

The lone adult, a raven-haired woman with fair skin and bright red lipstick, reached for her hand. "I'm Ms. Madison, their advisor. Thanks for having us."

After a brief conversation with Ms. Madison, Ainsley led her and her students around the operations suite, letting them ask questions about what they saw. The students briefly interacted with Duval and Kelly before she took them back to the lobby to await their audience with Gage.

When he appeared, he wore his sunglasses on top of his head and carried his briefcase and keys. "Good afternoon. I'm Gage Woodson, chief operations officer of 404 Sound." He waited for a beat as if expecting the kids to applaud or cheer. When they didn't, he spoke again, his tone somewhat annoyed. "Do any of you have any specific questions about what I do here?"

"Aren't you the founder's son?" a boy with blond-tipped dreadlocks asked.

Gage nodded. "404 is a family business. All the execs are my siblings."

"Then you probably don't do much. Since you can't get fired or nothing." The boy chuckled at his own cleverness.

Ms. Madison's reprimand was swift. "Andrew! That's rude and unacceptable behavior."

Gage made a face. Adjusting his sunglasses, he said, "I've got a pressing engagement. Nice to meet you. Stay in school and all that." With his jaw tighter than piano wire, he strode past everyone and left.

Ainsley, left in his wake, shook her head. *I don't believe he acted like that. They're just kids.*

Every time she started thinking Gage was perfect, he reminded her that he wasn't. She couldn't go on pining after a man who couldn't be bothered to engage with children. Because at the end of the day, it wasn't just about her. She had Cooper to think about.

Standing in line at the counter of Chef Rob's Caribbean Cafe and Upscale Lounge, Gage perused the menu in his hands. The restaurant's festive walls, painted in oranges and reds, hosted a collection of unique Jamaican-themed art. His father, Caleb, standing next to him, was engaged in the same hard process of choosing a meal from Chef Rob's many delicious offerings. There were quite a few people in line behind them, and Gage didn't want to hold them up. His father's voice cut into his thoughts. "Thanks for meeting me here, son."

"It's not a problem. I never pass up a chance to come down here and get some of those jerk egg rolls." He rubbed his stomach as an emphasis on the last few words. "Can't get them anywhere else."

Laughing to himself, Caleb returned his attention to his menu.

After they ordered, they seated themselves in one of the black leather–upholstered booths with their drinks. Gage set his phone to vibrate and laid it face-down on the table, as his father usually demanded. "So, what's the occasion, Dad?"

"Just checking in with you. I know you're headed to Cali in a few days to rendezvous with our equipment for Studio 1."

"Yep. I'm not taking any more chances that it will make it here safely." He sipped from his cup of lemonade. "I plan on spending that whole day making sure we're set for The Visionary's session."

"Excellent. I'm glad to see you're taking this seriously, Gage." Caleb rested his hands on the table, clasping his fingers. "Because we can't really afford any more mistakes."

He cringed because the words stung. But he brushed it off just as quickly as he felt it. "You're right, and I don't plan on making any more. That's why Ainsley and I are just making it a day trip. Fly there, get the equipment, be home by dark."

Caleb's brow hitched. "Ainsley?"

"Yeah, she's going with me. Everything pertaining to operations at 404 lives on her tablet. Taking her with me means all the electronic forms can be filled out that much faster, as well as the arrangements that need to be made for getting the equipment set up and operational in the studio."

"I'm not sure she absolutely needs to go with you."

"No, Dad, she doesn't absolutely need to. It will just make the process smoother and faster if she does." He frowned, wondering why his father was suddenly so concerned about the way he chose to run his department. "Is there a problem?"

Caleb sighed, but before he could open his mouth to say anything, their food was delivered. As the waitress set the Rasta Pasta in front of him, he smiled and offered her a polite thanks.

Gage did the same as he looked over his jerk egg rolls with shrimp and steamed red snapper. When the waitress was gone, he picked up his fork but continued to watch his father as he took his first few bites.

"Son, I know you don't like to talk about what happened between you and Tara…"

He felt his jaw tighten. "Then why bring it up? Unless you have news about the case."

"Because it's relevant to what we're talking about." Caleb took several bites of his pasta.

"I don't see how." *You're right, I don't want to talk about Tara.* The one time he'd broken his personal rule of not dating anyone who worked for the company, it had failed spectacularly.

"You let yourself get closer to her than you should have, and it backfired, big-time." Caleb paused. "Normally I wouldn't come down on you about it, but since the company took a financial hit because of your actions, I can't overlook it."

He scoffed. *I got close to her. I loved her. Or at least, I thought I did.* She'd been duplicitous, conniving. She'd used his affections against him. "What does that have to do with the price of tea in China?

There's nothing like that going on between Ainsley and me."

"For now." Caleb continued eating, with that same knowing, fatherly look on his face that he always had when he just knew he was right about something.

Gage sighed. "Look. I'll admit that Ainsley is attractive." *Gorgeous, if I'm being honest. No need to tell him that.* "But I've got more self-control than that. Besides, it's just a quick day trip."

Caleb shrugged. "That's what you have planned. But in all my years of living, I've learned things rarely go according to our plans, son."

Shaking his head, he decided to concentrate on his food rather than continue this fruitless conversation. He kept quiet until he'd cleaned his plate and finished his drink.

"You can't ignore the truth in what I'm saying, Gage. I know you don't like to hear it, but I tell you these things for your own good. Any father worth his salt would."

"I understand your concerns. But, as I said, there's absolutely nothing between us."

Caleb cocked his head to the right. "You're honestly going to sit here and say that, as if I've never seen the way you look at her?"

He frowned. "What? When?"

"Company-wide meetings. On more than one occasion, I've seen you watching her."

"Yikes. That's what you're doing during those meetings?"

His father shrugged. "What can I say? After all these years, meetings aren't terribly exciting anymore, so I take my entertainment where I can get it."

"Really, Dad?" He tossed a balled-up paper napkin at his old man.

Batting the crumpled paper away, Caleb laughed. "In all seriousness, it's hard not to notice. And I've seen her looking at you as well."

That gave him pause. *Is he telling the truth, or is he just heaping on in an attempt to prove that he's right?*

"All I'm saying is, be careful. Try not to let this business trip turn into something more complex between the two of you."

"I hear you."

"I hope so."

Gage thought of Ainsley and couldn't help smiling. She was professional, efficient and gorgeous. Beyond that, she had a magical way of cracking a joke at just the right moment to keep him from going off the deep end. Everyone who crossed her path loved her—she was definitely the glue that held his department together. *No, I know better than to start anything with her.* "Listen, since you brought up Tara, where are we with the case? Do you have news?"

"I do. Our investigator located Tara just outside Cleveland, but she claims to have spent the money on medical treatments for her nephew."

He cursed. "What now? Do we sue her? Will she go to jail?"

Caleb shook his head. "Your mother and I, along with Nia, decided to drop the charges."

"What? Why?"

"Her sister is a single mother of a young child who has a lot of health problems." Caleb ran a hand over his face. "I'm not saying that justifies what Tara did. But our attorney said the likelihood of us ever getting any restitution from Tara was slim to none."

"I don't care. I'll bring my own case against her. She has to face some kind of consequences." His ex-girlfriend had run off with ten stacks of company funds, and he wouldn't let her get away with it. The only thing she'd lost was her job in the finance department. Meanwhile, he'd suffered a much greater loss: he'd lost his father's faith in him. He wouldn't let that happen again.

No. There's no way I can get involved with Ainsley. I know she's not the same as Tara but dating someone at work just isn't going to go well. He just couldn't take the chance. Not now, and not ever again.

Five

Just after seven Monday morning, Ainsley watched over Cooper as he made his last-minute preparations for the school day. "Come on, son. You should be headed to the bus stop."

"I know, I know." He dashed up the stairs.

"Grab a jacket while you're up there!" She waited at the bottom of the stairs for him to return, all the while with the front door propped open. If the bus pulled up before he returned, she could flag down the driver and signal him that they needed a minute.

He jogged back down the stairs then, with his book bag strap in one hand and a jacket slung over the arm.

She furrowed her brow. "Cooper, it's chilly out. Put the jacket *on*."

"You said to grab a jacket," he groused. "Can't I just take it with me?"

She sighed. Many of the mothers with sons on the baseball team often commiserated about their kids' apparent allergy to outerwear. *What is it with boys and not wanting to wear jackets? Why do they insist on being cold needlessly?* "It's not gonna do you any good to carry it, child. Put the jacket on. You can take it off once you're inside the school."

He frowned, his small lips pursed tight, but slipped into the jacket anyway.

"Thank you." She leaned down and kissed his forehead. "I'll see you when I get back from California this evening, okay? Make sure you do as Bebe says while I'm gone."

"I got it, Mom." He slipped his book bag straps over his shoulders, mumbling something.

She knew what he'd said, but she couldn't resist teasing him just a little bit. "What was that?" She cupped her hand around her ear.

"Love you," he repeated as he ran out the front door.

"Love you, too," she called after him. He reached the curb just as the bus pulled up. She watched him get on, then watched the bus pull away.

Closing the door, she climbed the stairs. In her bedroom, she touched up her makeup and shrugged into a tan cardigan over the simple burgundy midi dress she wore. Back downstairs, she grabbed her purse and keys, along with the bag of supplies she'd packed up for the trip, and left. Tucking her things into her car, she walked across her driveway and over to Bebe's house next door.

The Redfords had been her neighbors for seven years, since she and Eden first bought the house. Bebe was short for Beatrice. She ran a marketing company from home, while her husband, Fitz, worked at a car dealership in the city.

Bebe answered after the second knock. She was petite and fair-skinned, with close-trimmed red hair. Clad in gray leggings, a green tunic and dinosaur-feet slippers, she had a steaming mug of coffee in one hand. "Morning, Ainsley. Ready for your trip?"

She nodded. "I think so. As long as my boss doesn't make any last-minute demands, I should be good."

"Great. Do you wanna come in, have a cup of coffee?"

"I can't. We're supposed to be wheels up in less than an hour, and I still have to make it to the airport." She reached out, giving Bebe a quick hug around the shoulders. "Thanks again for looking after Cooper for me."

"No problem, honey. Have a safe trip." With a wink and a smile, Bebe shut her door.

Hopping in her car, Ainsley made her way across town to DeKalb-Peachtree Airport. The route took her east on I-20 then northeast on I-85, cutting right through the heart of downtown Atlanta. As she braved the morning traffic, she watched the beautiful scenery of her hometown passing by her windows. *Even though the commute's a killer, I still love this place.* She couldn't imagine living anywhere else.

When she finally arrived at the private airstrip used by 404, she pulled her car into one of the five parking spots and got out. There was only one other car there, and it wasn't Gage's. Assuming it was the pilot's, she got her things out of the car and headed for the plane. Impressed with the design of the company's recently upgraded jet, she admired the brightly colored logo paint job on the fuselage. The door was open, and the stairs were in place, so she boarded.

She gasped as she entered. The interior was even more impressive than the exterior. Four spacious leather seats were placed on either side of the aisle. In the rear, a minibar and a booth-like conferencing area had been set up. There were two flat-screen televisions, one in the front and one in the rear. Moving to the minibar, she opened the cabinet and fridge, placing Gage's snacks and drinks in their appropriate places.

"Ainsley. It's been a long time since I've seen you."

Turning toward the sound of the familiar female voice, Ainsley smiled when she saw Max coming out of the cockpit. "Hey, Max. How have you been?"

"Can't complain. Especially since the Woodsons

upgraded me to this swanky bird. She's a beauty, isn't she?"

"Definitely." She chuckled.

"I call her the Swingin' Ms. D." Max rubbed her hands together.

"Oh, after Dinah Washington."

Max looked impressed. "I see you know your jazz greats. Yeah, she's just like Dinah. Curvy and sophisticated and moves like a dream." With a smile, she disappeared back into her domain at the controls.

Taking the front window seat on the right side of the jet, Ainsley settled in and fastened her seat belt. A quick glance at her phone showed the time. *Where's Gage? He's the one who suggested this eight thirty departure time.* She thought about calling him but decided not to. *He's grown, and he knows where he's supposed to be.*

Pulling her tablet from her purse, she opened the file with the urban fantasy novel she'd been reading. She had a four-and-a-half-hour flight ahead of her, and if she kept reading, she expected to finish the book by the time they got to California.

She'd just flipped the page when Gage rushed onto the plane, carrying his small attaché. He'd dressed in a tan suit with a crisp white shirt beneath and no tie. His sunglasses were nestled in his riotous curls. "Morning, Ainsley. I see you beat me here."

"I didn't want to hold you up."

"I appreciate that. I trust all my supplies are here?"

"Already put away in the minibar."

"Thanks." He tossed his case into the seat across the aisle from her and walked back to the minibar.

She followed his movement, her eyes resting on his firm-looking backside and powerful thighs. She swallowed, her throat suddenly dry. "Would you pass me a bottle of water, please?"

"Sure." He handed her the water as he returned to his seat with one of his coffee-infused smoothies and a protein bar. Twisting off the cap, he raised the bottle in her direction. "Here's to a great flight."

She lifted her water bottle. "Cheers." That said, she broke the seal, tossed the cap aside and took a healthy swig. She always felt like this whenever she and Gage were in an enclosed space together. That was why she avoided this scenario whenever possible. Within the confines of the private jet, though, there was nowhere to hide from his intoxicating presence.

She shook her head, returning her attention to her book. *The best thing I can do is just read the whole way. I'll start the next book in the series on the flight back.* For a few moments, she had herself convinced that she'd give her full attention to the book for the duration of the flight.

By the time they were in the air, though, she couldn't ignore him anymore.

She hazarded a glance in his direction...

And found him watching her.

* * *

I should really be doing some work. So why can't I focus?

Gage already knew the answer to that. His proximity to Ainsley made concentration damn near impossible. If they had to share a workspace this size in the 404 building, he'd probably be way less productive.

Gage spent a few more seconds staring at Ainsley. She was wearing a burgundy dress with a pair of matching heels. Her hair was up in a high bun atop her head, and her trusty stylus was nestled in her hair. Cradling her tablet on her lap, her eyes scanned the pages of the book she read.

Suddenly she looked up.

Yikes. Caught. There was no way he could hide the fact that he'd been watching her, so he didn't try. "Sorry," he murmured.

"It's fine. Is there something you need?"

He shook his head. "No."

She returned her attention to the book, and he pulled his laptop out of his attaché case. Opening it up, he turned it on and pulled up the word processor file he'd been using to write his speech for the company's thirtieth anniversary. While he still had time, he didn't want to wait until the last minute to come up with something.

Max's voice came over the intercom. "Buckle up, folks. We may be hitting some turbulence in the next few minutes."

He tightened his belt in response to Max's advice, then went back to his document. Reading over the few paragraphs he'd written so far, he scratched his chin. His parents were expecting each sibling to give a five-minute speech at the upcoming anniversary gala, and he was having a hard time deciding what he wanted to say.

I suppose it's less about what I want to say than it is what's appropriate to say. He wanted his speech to be profound yet entertaining, a look at the company's history as well as its future. *I bet Nia's speech has been done for ages. She always knows what to say at these events.* His eldest sister, CEO of the company and apple of her parents' eyes, never missed an opportunity to make them proud.

He stared at the words on the page for several minutes, making tweaks here and there until the words started to blur together. The plane shook then as they hit a pocket of rough air, and the computer rattled on the tray table. He steadied it, then shut it down and stowed it safely in his bag. *Better to put it away now than risk having to replace it.*

Ainsley kept reading, seemingly unfazed.

Things evened out again, and he settled his back against his seat and pulled out his phone. Even with it in airplane mode, there were still a few odds and ends he could tie up. So he opened his notes app and started typing into it.

He'd typed barely four words before the plane began shaking again, this time much harder than before. He gripped the phone a bit tighter. He glanced across the aisle at Ainsley. She was wide-eyed, clutching her tablet to her chest.

It subsided a few minutes later. When the aircraft ceased its trembling, he asked, "You okay over there?"

She nodded. "Fine. Just…not a fan of turbulence."

He chuckled. "I don't think anybody enjoys being rattled around in their seat like that."

Her answering laugh sounded nervous. "Fair enough."

He tucked his phone away for the same reason he'd put away his computer. It was almost as if the universe were advising him to set work aside for now. "Do you want me to come over and sit with you? You know, in case the turbulence happens again. We can help guard each other's electronics."

She laughed again, the sound a little less strained. She moved her purse from the seat next to her and set it on the floor. "Sure, that's fine."

Securing his attaché case inside the under-seat storage drawer, he moved over to sit in the aisle seat next to her. After he buckled up and settled in, he asked, "Ever been to Cali before?"

She shook her head. "No. Never been any farther west than Las Vegas."

"I see. It's been about a year since I went the last time." He gestured to the tablet, still pinned to her chest by her crossed arms. "I think you can put that down now."

She closed the cover over her tablet and laid it across her lap, resting her arm on it. She opened her mouth, but before she could speak, a loud boom of thunder sounded.

"Oh boy." He felt the tension gathering in his shoulders. This trip had a tight turnaround, and he didn't have time for any delays. "I'm gonna need this weather to calm down so we can get this equipment back to Atlanta on time."

A familiar, steady sound filled the cabin.

She turned away to slide up the plastic shade covering the window. Fat droplets of rain pelted the window, and a flash of lightning illuminated the cloud-shrouded sky. "Looks like Mother Nature might have other plans."

"Well, that sucks." He felt his brow furrowing as the familiar frustration sank its fingers into his flesh.

"When it rains like this, I remember how obsessed Cooper was with jumping in rain puddles when he was younger." She laughed softly. "Regular rain boots wouldn't work for him because he always went for the deepest puddles he could find. Do you know how hard it was to find kid-size hip waders for my little munchkin?"

"I can't imagine." And he couldn't. He could count on one hand the number of times he'd interacted with a small child, and he didn't feel deprived of anything because of it.

Max's voice came over the intercom again. "I'm sorry to report, the storm has suddenly switched course. I don't have enough fuel payload to go around it, so we're going to have to make a surprise landing."

He blew out a breath. "Perfect."

"Maybe we won't have to stay too long." Ainsley crossed, then uncrossed her legs. "We can just pop into town, grab a bite, then be back in the air."

He knew she was trying to lighten the mood, and he appreciated that. But he wasn't sure anything could improve his mood in the face of this unexpected delay.

"Okay, last announcement. We'll be landing in about twenty minutes in a little town called Summer Village, Louisiana." Maxine paused. "Right on the Louisiana and Arkansas border."

He sighed. Not only were they making a landing, but it also seemed they were going to be way off the beaten path. "Ever heard of this place, Ainsley?"

She shook her head.

"Neither have I. I'm guessing it's not that big of a place."

As the plane went into the descent, he leaned back in his seat. She did the same, her hand gripping the armrest between them. Seeing the white in her knuckles, he quietly laid his hand atop hers.

She gasped softly, but he could feel her tension subsiding under his touch.

Neither of them said a word, but their eyes remained locked.

The interaction was totally innocent, but he felt the tingle moving through him as he touched her.

He'd merely sought to comfort her and had managed to reawaken his desire for her in the process.

I could be the one who does this for her. I could be the one who comforts her when she's upset or afraid. Where did that thought come from? *This is a business trip. Business only.*

Six

Ainsley watched out the window as their plane taxied down the remote airstrip. There wasn't much in the way of scenery, just the sheets of rain, the gray skies and a few distant trees.

As they neared a large, barnlike structure, a man in overalls appeared, opening the doors wide. She undid her seat belt as the jet slowly rolled inside the cavernous building.

Next to her, Gage got to his feet. He was getting his things from beneath the seat when they came to a stop.

Inside the hangar, the sounds of the rain and thunder became somewhat muffled.

Max opened the cabin door and stood in the center

of the aisle. "Well, we made it to Summer Village. I'm sorry. I thought we'd be ahead of the storm, but it turned at the last minute. We hit the outer edge."

"That's the outer edge? I'd hate to hit it full-on." Ainsley's eyes widened at the thought.

"The real question is, how long are we going to be here?" Gage gripped the strap of his attaché case.

"Depends on the weather." Max ran a hand over her chin. "At least overnight, based on what I know right now. Hopefully, the storm lets up so we can get underway tomorrow."

"Yikes." Ainsley reached for her phone. "I have to call Bebe and let her know I won't be home tonight." Holding her phone up, she started to make the call, then frowned. "Crap. No signal."

Max chuckled. "We're inside a barn in the middle of nowhere, and there's like a hundred percent cloud cover. You're gonna have to hold off on the call."

Ainsley sighed.

Gage scowled. "Damn. Looks like we'll be needing lodging for the night, then."

Ainsley watched his expression and could tell he was annoyed by the inconvenience. *At least he's doing a decent job of controlling it.* She knew no one else understood his moods the way she did.

"Let me get the stairs down and you two can get off." Maxine walked past them to the rear of the aisle, behind where Gage had originally been sitting.

Ainsley's brow furrowed. "'You two'? What about you, Max?"

"I'm staying with my baby," she remarked as she opened the doors and prepared their exit route. "I'll be fine on the jet until we can get underway again. Besides, I need to secure her and supervise her refueling."

"You folks coming out?" A man's voice called.

The three of them deplaned, meeting the man in overalls who'd opened the doors at the foot of the stairs.

"Hey, y'all." The man, with his ruddy complexion, shaggy brown hair and blue eyes offered them a friendly smile. "Hugh Delmar, at your service."

"Kidder, pilot." Max shook Hugh's hand. "Thanks for letting me in here."

"This storm hit fast and out of nowhere. It ain't fit weather out there for man nor beast, so you're welcome to this old barn as long as you need it. When I heard you over the radio, I knew this was your only good place to land." Hugh turned toward Gage. "And you are…"

"Gage Woodson, chief operations officer at 404 Sound in Atlanta. And this is my assistant, Ainsley."

"Whew, boy. You said a mouthful. Pleased to meet ya, Mr. Woodson." Hugh chuckled softly, then looked to her. "And you too, Miss Ainsley."

"Likewise, Mr. Delmar."

"Welcome to Summer Village, folks." He tipped his ratty old baseball cap in their direction.

"Thanks. Could you point us toward a local

hotel?" She watched him expectantly. "Preferably one with a shuttle."

"Oh, there's no hotels here. Not for a good fifty miles or so. The only place to stay is the Duchess Bed and Breakfast."

Gage frowned. "Really?"

"'Fraid so." Hugh started walking toward the open doors. "I can carry you over there if you want, though I can only fit two of you in my truck."

Max waved him off, already going back up the stairs. "No problem. I'm staying with my jet."

"All right. If you need anything, you can use the old landline phone in my office over there. I still do woodwork out of this barn from time to time." As Max disappeared into the jet, Hugh said, "Ready, folks?"

Shielding herself with her tote bag, Ainsley dashed out into the rain behind the two men. Once she was loaded into the cab of Hugh's old pickup truck, seated between the two of them, she settled in for the ride.

The two men talked over her the whole time, with Hugh asking questions and Gage answering in the same clipped tone he always used when he was upset about something. She opted out of any questions directed at her by shrugging. Gage cut his eyes at her a few times, but she ignored him.

About twenty minutes later, they rolled past a sign announcing their arrival in town. The cluster of businesses along both sides of the main street, along with the old-fashioned streetlights that resembled old gas lamps, could only be described as charming. The relentless rain continued to fall.

The truck turned down a rutted road and drove about a mile before coming to a stop in front of a two-story house. The white structure, with its bright green shutters and the rockers sitting on the wide wraparound porch, resembled an old plantation house.

They got out and ran up on the porch, struggling to dodge the rain. Inside the open door, they approached the tall desk where a woman stood.

Hugh greeted the woman. "How's it going, Mary?"

"Can't complain." The woman tucked a lock of her blond hair behind her ear. "Brought me some guests?"

"Sure did. They stashed their plane in my barn. Got a room for them?"

"Last one." Mary fished around beneath her desk and pulled out a key with a bright pink tag labeled with the number four. "It's your lucky night, folks."

"We're gonna need two rooms," Gage interjected.

Mary cringed. "Oh, honey. We only have the one real room."

Ainsley asked, "What do you mean by that?"

"I mean we've got a single bed set up in the basement, but we only rent that out in emergencies."

Gage pulled out his wallet. "I'll take the basement."

"You sure? It's nothing fancy, and it can get a little damp and drafty down there. That's why we don't rent it out much." Mary watched Gage's face.

"I'm sure it'll be fine. I'll take the basement room." He slid his gold card across the desk.

Mary smiled, a knowing look on her face. "Whatever you say." She retrieved a second key, this one with a green tag attached. "Breakfast is from seven to nine. Miss, your room's upstairs, first door on the right." She passed the pink key to Ainsley, and the green one to Gage. "I'll show you downstairs to yours."

"Gotcha." He pocketed the key. "So, what's the Wi-Fi password here? I'd like to finish up some work, and all my stuff is in the cloud."

Her brow hitched, Mary replied, "There's a computer in the corner of the breakfast room you can use. It's wired for the internet. No Wi-Fi. Sorry, sugar."

Gage sighed. "Thanks for your help."

Watching for a moment as Mary led him away, Ainsley trudged up the stately stairs with her tote bag tucked under her arm.

With his attaché case in hand, Gage followed Mary through the lobby, past the dining room and through the farmhouse kitchen. The kitchen, with its cream wallpaper printed with cherries, reminded him of his great-grandmother's home down in Shreveport. Reaching a door set in the rearmost wall, she gestured to it. "Here it is." Inserting the key into the lock, Gage opened the door to the room. Glancing around, he sighed. A darkness-shrouded staircase lay before him, and to his mind, it looked like the descent into a cave.

"Hold on, hon. Let me get the light." Mary reached around him and flipped a switch.

A dim, yellowish light illuminated the staircase, which descended for several steps before the next landing, where it veered off to the right.

"Watch your step. The stairs are a little crooked in places." Mary walked ahead of him.

The two of them walked down slowly, and he detected the aroma of damp earth filling his nostrils. When they reached the landing, Mary stopped short.

He walked into her. "Sorry."

"Well, fiddlesticks." Mary shook her head. "Looks like this terrible weather has done us in."

Looking down the next flight of stairs, he saw what she was referring to. The entire basement was flooded, and from his position, he couldn't determine the depth of standing water. Only three steps below where they stood were above water, the rest of the space resembling a man-made lake.

"Yikes." Looking to his left, he could see the rectangular glass window around which the water continued to stream in.

"Dang it. I thought we'd sealed up that window leak." Mary whistled. "Well, unless you've got a wet suit and scuba gear in that bag, I don't think you'll be able to sleep down here, Mr. Woodsby."

"Woodson," he corrected. "And no, I don't." He watched a few tools and knickknacks float by before turning and going back up the stairs and through the kitchen.

Mary met him at the front desk. "Sorry about that. You probably wouldn't have been too comfortable in the basement anyway, but I apologize for the inconvenience."

He shrugged. "It couldn't be helped." *I guess I'll be headed back to the barn to crash on the jet. Hopefully, Max won't mind the company.* "Where's Ainsley's room again? I need to let her know what happened."

"She's in room four. It's right by the stairs—you can't miss it." Mary winked.

Unsure of what the innkeeper was getting at, he turned and headed up the stairs. Knocking on the door, he waited.

She opened it a few seconds later. "Gage? I thought you were taking the basement room?"

He shook his head. "The place is more suited for swimming than sleeping right now. It's flooded."

"Oh crap." Her brow furrowed, her expression concerned. "What are you going to do?"

"Head back over to the barn and crash on the jet with Max. I just came up here to let you know."

She shook her head. "No. You shouldn't have to go back out in this awful weather. Why don't you just share this room with me?"

He swallowed, thinking about what she'd offered him.

"I mean, I'm sure the front desk has a rollaway bed or a cot or something."

"I hadn't thought about that, but I guess we can check." He scratched his chin.

She stepped back. "Come on in. You can use the phone to call the desk so you don't have to go back down."

He entered the room and looked around while she closed the door behind him. The accommodations were nowhere near as posh as he usually preferred, but he supposed that was to be expected in middle-of-nowhere, Louisiana. Moving inside the room, he shrugged out of his damp sport coat. "Whew, that's better. I was roasting."

"If the room had two doubles, it wouldn't be an issue. Unfortunately, there's only one bed," Ainsley remarked, pointing.

He looked where she indicated, well aware of the sarcasm in her tone. Sure enough, the room had one queen-size bed, dressed in an extremely floral bedding ensemble. "Looks that way." One corner of the room held two plush-looking armchairs and a coffee table, situated around a small fireplace. He went to the bedside table and picked up the phone, dialing zero for the front desk. "Hi, Mary. This is Gage Woodson. Would you happen to have any rollaway beds?"

"Sure, we've got one. I'll have someone bring it up to you this evening."

"Thanks." He hung up. "Someone will bring a rollaway up later."

She shook her head as she walked past him, dropping her purse on the coffee table. "I hope it's a decent-size one. It'd take some origami-level folding for you to sleep in one of those little beds."

"So...you're offering to sleep in the rollaway, then?"

She shrugged. "We can decide when they bring it up."

He tossed his attaché case on the bed. "What are we going to do now? Without Wi-Fi, the choices are pretty limited." Heavy rain still fell outside, and the sound, which usually soothed him, didn't seem to be working this time around.

She shrugged. "My first priority right now is getting in contact with Bebe. She needs to know I won't be home tonight since she's looking after Cooper." Slipping out of her shoes, she flopped down in one of the chairs and pulled out her phone.

He groaned inwardly. This entire trip had gone way off the rails. He'd been so determined to make this process quick and seamless. Get on the plane, get to Cali, grab the equipment and get it back to the studio. Now, thanks to Mother Nature, an industrial-size wrench had been thrown in his plans.

And then there was Ainsley. After spending so long trying his best to keep his distance, now he'd be forced to share this tiny room with her. How was he supposed to focus? She was so beautiful; it made his eyes hurt to look at her sometimes. Still, he couldn't help admiring her. So, he stood there, watching her, unable to look away.

Finally, she looked up from her phone. "Um, didn't you have some work to do?"

The question made him cringe, because it felt like outright dismissal. "I did."

"Looks like you get to avail yourself of the inn's 'state-of-the-art' business center, then." She winked.

He cut his eyes at her, not amused at her little quip. "I'll be back."

"Cool. I'll hang out here reading my book, hoping the weather changes." She went back to her phone call.

Stretching his arms above his head to release some of the tension in his shoulders, he picked up his attaché case from the bed and left the room.

Back downstairs, he found Mary seated behind the desk, flipping through a magazine. She looked up as he approached. "Something you need, Mr. Woodsby?"

"That's Woodson," he corrected her. "And yes. I'm going to need to use the computer."

Her brow furrowed. "Might want to make it quick, sugar. The weather report says the storm's bound to intensify, and if it starts lightning and thundering again, I'm gonna have to shut that thing off."

"I'm sorry, what?"

"We don't run unnecessary electronics when it's storming, sugar." She watched him with a curious expression. "Where'd you say you're from?"

"I didn't, but I'm from Atlanta."

She chuckled. "Ain't you ever had a granny? You should know the drill."

He smiled despite his annoyance, because her words reminded him of his paternal grandmother's insistence on total darkness and silence in her house during a thunderstorm.

She gestured to her right. "The computer's in that back corner, right next to the window seat."

"Thanks." He walked through the breakfast area, with its striped wallpaper, dark wood tables and chairs, and aged mauve carpet, until he reached the large picture window that took up the majority of the rear wall. A window seat, complete with a floral cushion, was positioned just beneath it.

The window, dressed in gauzy, sheer white curtains, gave a view of the grassy knoll behind the inn, as well as the dense forest beyond. He imagined the window provided a lot of sunlight to the space on a nice day. Today, though, there was only the gray skies, the rain hitting the glass pane and the trees swaying in the wind.

To the right of the window sat a small writing desk, upon which a less-than-current desktop computer sat. He pulled out the chair, setting his case on the window seat as he sat in the chair by the desk. Pressing the power button, he watched as the aged machine roared to life, with fans whirring. Finally, it booted up fully, and he opened the internet browser to access his personal document cloud.

When he'd finished going through reports and interoffice memos, he shut the computer down and tucked his handwritten notes back into his case. As he passed the desk, he nodded to Mary before heading up the stairs.

Approaching their door, he could hear Ainsley talking. He paused.

"No, he went to use the computer. He's too work-obsessed to just chill for a minute, you know what I mean?" She paused, then laughed.

He felt his jaw tighten. *She doesn't even know me well enough to say something like that. She sees me working because that's the only place she sees me—at the office.* And why should he be blamed for being competent and hardworking anyway? Somebody had to make sure things got done. He rolled his eyes.

"Well, I'm not gonna keep you on the line all day. Since you've got Cooper's key, you can get into the house if he needs anything. Okay, girl. I'll talk to you later."

If only I could shake these pesky feelings for her. Then I wouldn't care what she thought of me.

He wanted her, and it seemed the more he tried to deny his feelings, the more they rose to the surface. Logic and common sense told him time and again that he simply couldn't risk being in another relationship right now, especially one with a coworker.

My ex accused me of being too work focused. Repeatedly. Oddly enough, she'd leveraged that insult to get him to drop his guard so she could swindle the company. He shook his head. Nope. He wasn't going to let his feelings get the better of him. Not this time.

Seven

Ainsley had just pocketed her phone when Gage walked in. Looking his way, she asked, "Did you finish your work?"

"Yeah." His answer was curt, gruff.

She frowned. *What's the matter with him?* Deciding not to engage with his bad mood, she fished her tablet out of her purse. "It's a little after one our time. Do you want me to get lunch now, or should we get an early dinner in a few hours? Because I'm going to take a nap."

"Early dinner after a nap." She watched him kick off his shoes, drop his attaché on the nightstand and fall onto the bed face-first. Shrugging, she went back to the book she'd been trying to read on the plane.

The story, set on a distant planet and featuring some pretty cool fantasy elements, held her attention pretty well under most circumstances. But, with her handsome boss lying just feet away from her, snoring softly, she found herself distracted from the tale. She kept looking up, stealing glances at his sleeping form. Her eyes raked over his body, noting the way the fabric of his dress shirt stretched over the muscles of his arms, the way his back rose and fell in time with his breaths, even the way his slacks clung to his backside.

She swallowed. *Have mercy.*

Tearing her eyes away, she went back to her book. Two hours later, she'd had it. There was simply no good way to focus on reading with a man that fine so close by. So she grabbed her cardigan, which had dried somewhat since they arrived, and slipped it on along with her shoes. Grabbing her purse, she quietly left the room, so as not to wake him as she exited.

Once downstairs, she called Max to get an update on the weather. Although it had slowed here, it was raging along their flight path. They were definitely staying put for the night. Max was safe in the barn with the jet. Ainsley told her to help herself to any of the food in the little fridge.

At the desk, Ainsley spoke briefly with the innkeeper so she could borrow an umbrella. She remembered having seen a diner among the businesses they'd passed, so with the borrowed umbrella and the bright yellow poncho Mary had insisted she use, she made her way outside and started walking. The rain was steady but not as bad as before. If she was going to make a run for food, now was the time.

It took less than ten minutes to make it to the main road, and that was only because she took care to avoid puddles and patches of slick mud. When she stepped onto the sidewalk on Main Street, she made a beeline for the blue-and-white-striped awning she'd seen earlier.

She let down her umbrella beneath the awning, then opened the door to the Blue Rose Diner. Inside, she left the umbrella near the door and took a good look around. The cream-colored wallpaper was emblazoned with the diner's namesake flower, and the chairs at the small round tables all had blue cushions.

Walking up to the counter, she smiled at the two people she saw behind it. There was a man and a woman, both dressed in blue with black aprons. "Hey, there."

"Welcome to the Blue Rose, little lady." The man, tall and dark-skinned, wore a cook's cap that matched his apron. Touching a long-handled spatula to the edge of his cap in salute, he said, "I'm Bud. This is my wife, Rose. She'll get your order."

Rose, a petite, caramel-skinned lady whose dark hair was streaked with gray, smiled in her direction. "Need a minute to look over the menu, honey?"

"Yes, thanks." She looked up at the menu board above the counter. It was an old-fashioned board, with black plastic letters and numbers stuck to a ridged surface to spell out the place's offerings and prices. It took her a few minutes to find something she thought Gage would eat, and once she settled on that, she ordered. "I'll be taking this to-go. Let me get the grilled chicken salad, no dairy, no carbs, with fat-free dressing on the side."

"Goodness. That's pretty much just lettuce, tomato and cucumber, honey. Are you sure that's all you want?"

She held back a laugh. "Oh, that's not for me, that's for my boss. He's very health-conscious."

"I see." Rose punched the order into the register. "What are you gonna have?"

"Let me get a bacon cheeseburger, well-done, with fries. And two drinks."

"A woman after my own heart." Rose grinned as she entered the rest of the order and gave her the total.

Handing over the cash plus an extra five, Ainsley said, "Keep the change." She walked to the tall, glass-front refrigerator next to the counter and chose a cola for herself and a bottle of water for Gage. Moving to one of the tables by the front windows, she sat down to wait for the food. While she waited, she pulled out her phone. The signal wasn't great, but it was enough for her to do a bit of scrolling down her social media feeds.

"Your food's ready, honey." Rose's voice cut into her thoughts.

Putting her phone away, she returned to the counter to get the large plastic bag containing her order.

"Napkins and everything are already in there." Rose held out the bag. "You enjoy, and come back and see us, okay?"

"Thanks." Tucking the drinks inside, she accepted the bag. With the food in hand, and her purse slung over her shoulder, she grabbed the borrowed umbrella, opening it as she stepped back outside. The chill in the air touched her right away, and she hustled back to the hotel as quickly as she could while avoiding the pitfalls of the wet terrain. The last thing she wanted to do was take a fall and ruin their meal before they even got a chance to enjoy it. *Though I don't know how much enjoyment Gage is gonna get out of this plain-ass salad anyway.* Giggling to herself, she climbed onto the inn's porch.

Inside, she returned the umbrella and the poncho to Mary, then climbed the stairs. When she opened the door, she found Gage sitting on the edge of the bed, flipping channels on the television. "Oh, there you are. I was going to call you."

"While the rain slowed, I thought I'd grab us an early dinner." She closed the door behind her and sat the bag of food down on the bed.

"Where'd you end up going?"

"We passed a diner on the way in, and I grabbed us food from there."

He looked skeptical.

She rolled her eyes. "I know what you eat and

what you don't, Gage. Remember, I've been ordering your lunches for years now." She checked the foam trays, removing his and handing it over. "I got you a grilled chicken salad. Fat-free dressing on the side."

"No dairy and no carbs?" he asked as he took the tray.

"And no flavor," she added wryly, handing over his bottled water.

"Very funny." He opened the tray and inspected the contents. "Thanks, Ainsley."

"I'd say it was my pleasure, but I don't typically enjoy running around in the rain." As she took out her own tray and walked over to her chair, it occurred to her that if she didn't care about Gage, she wouldn't have subjected herself to the monsoon outside just to get him something to eat. That wasn't a thought she wanted to dwell on, so she decided to focus on her burger and fries instead.

They ate in relative silence while a home-improvement program played on the television. The burger, well-seasoned and cooked just right, tasted amazing, as did the crisp fries. By the time she finished her food and most of her drink, she berated herself for not having a nap earlier. Stifling a yawn, she got up and started collecting her trash, stuffing it back into the plastic bag. "You done?"

"Yes, thanks." Barely taking his attention off the television, he handed her his trash.

She opened the door and set the bag of trash in the hallway before closing it again. Walking to the window, she looked out at the stormy sky and wondered what the night ahead might hold.

Gage reclined on the bed, half watching the home improvement show on the television. While the host went on about shiplap and concrete countertops, he was busy stealing glances at Ainsley.

She'd taken out her tablet and was now engrossed in the story she was reading. Artfully arranged in the armchair, she had her legs draped over an arm, with her bare feet dangling side to side while she read. She looked so sexy, he had to look away, so he directed his gaze to the window instead.

Outside, the rain continued to fall at an increasing pace. He could hear the droplets hitting the roof, and it took him a minute to realize that the insistent thudding sound wasn't just rain. He got up, walking past Ainsley to the window. Looking outside, he could see the quarter-size pellets of hail whizzing by, along with the sheets of rain.

"Yikes. First the storm, now hail." He shook his head.

She glanced up from her tablet. "Let's hope it doesn't last. There's no way Max can get us out of here in a hailstorm."

He sighed. His grand plan of getting everything with the equipment settled in one day had effectively been flushed down the toilet. He'd been holding off on calling Harcroft, hoping that somehow this crazy weather would resolve in time for them to make it to California today. Resigned, he grabbed his phone and called them.

"I totally understand, Gage. However, I must advise that if you don't pick up your custom order within three business days, it will be placed up for sale."

Gage bristled. "You're kidding me, right?"

"Sorry, Gage. We have two additional custom orders that have come in, so we'll just divert our resources where they're needed."

By the time he hung up the phone, Gage was more frustrated than before. *Now I have to rush over there before they sell my equipment. What a colossal mess.*

He thrived on being in control, on having it all together. Yet everything about this situation had taken that power away from him. He dragged his open hand across his face, feeling the tension building in his neck and shoulders as he stood there.

"You okay, boss man?" Ainsley's voice cut through his thoughts.

He turned her way. "We've got a couple of days to get to Cali or Harcroft is going to sell our equipment and we'll be back at square one."

She cringed. "Oh crap."

"Yeah." He ran a hand over his hair. "I'm just stressed."

"I get it. But try not to let it get to you." She gestured toward the window. "It's the weather, something none of us have any control over. So, try not to beat yourself up about it."

He blew out a breath.

"Besides, I can't remember the last time I was out overnight. The circumstances aren't ideal, but at least I'm getting a break from mommy duties." She wiped the back of her hand across her brow, feigning exhaustion.

He chuckled. "Been that long, eh?" He couldn't even imagine the amount of work that went into raising a kid, let alone as a single parent with a demanding career.

She nodded. "I haven't been away from Cooper for more than a few hours since he was in like third grade." She shook her head. "My social life is barely viable."

"Technically it's still dead in the water." He winked. "Even though we're stranded, it's still a work trip."

She pursed her lips and blew a raspberry in his direction. "Thanks for the reminder, Mr. Killjoy."

He returned to the bed, grabbing the remote. "I suppose we might as well make the best of it. Redeem the time, as my granny used to say."

She closed the cover over her tablet. "How are we gonna do that? Do you have some kind of grand plan to bring my social life back from the dead?"

"Not in this weather. But we can at least watch a movie or two." He gestured toward the television screen. "The inn's cable provider has some pretty recent releases available on demand."

Before she could respond, a knock sounded on the

door. Opening it, Ainsley stepped aside so a young man could roll in the folded bed. A clear plastic bag containing bed linens sat atop it. Once it was in place between the queen bed and the window, the young man excused himself.

Tucking away her tablet, she joined Gage, sitting next to him on the foot of the bed. "Let's look through and see what they have."

They perused the selection of movies for a few minutes, each choosing a movie. Ainsley picked a gritty thriller with a sci-fi twist, one that left them both scratching their heads. Gage chose next, settling on a recent buddy-cop dramedy. The film was just as funny as the reviews suggested, and by the time it ended, they were both lying across the bed, laughing out loud.

He turned toward her, watching the way amusement softened her expression. "That was hilarious."

"You're telling me." Still laughing, she wiped the tears from her eyes. "I can't believe how raunchy it was."

He had to agree. There'd been more than a few off-color jokes and plenty of innuendos. "Good thing we're both mature adults."

"That depends on the day." She sat up then, tossing one long leg over the other. Stifling a yawn, she announced, "I'm tired."

He stood. "I can take a cue. Time for me to set up the rollaway." He walked over, unfolded the metal frame and used the linen in the bag to make up the bed. With that done, he looked it over. "It's not fancy, but at least it's big enough. I should be able to fit in it just fine."

She nodded. "Looks like it."

He eased out of his shirt then, revealing the white tank beneath. Once he was down to the tank and his boxers, he lay across the bed. Taking a moment to adjust his positioning, he found that no matter what he did, his feet dangled off the end just a bit. *No big deal.* The bed was comfortable, though it felt a bit on the lumpy side. He eyed the flat pillow, shaking his head. Picking it up, he manipulated it in his hands to redistribute the fibers inside. "If you're tired, I won't keep you up. Good night, Ainsley."

She offered a soft smile. "'Night, Gage."

"Shit."

The softly uttered curse woke Ainsley, and she sat up in bed. Years of motherhood had trained her to be a light sleeper, just in case Cooper needed something in the middle of the night.

The next sound she heard in the inky darkness was a sharp inhale, the sound of air being sucked in through clenched teeth. Blinking against the blackness, she said, "Gage? Are you all right?"

"I think I might be bleeding." His reply was tinged with pain.

"Bleeding?" Reaching for the bedside lamp, she clicked it on. In the yellow glow, she looked toward

Gage, and found him sitting up on the edge of the rollaway bed. "Where?"

He cringed. "My back." He turned at the waist.

Her eyes widened as she saw the rather large snag, as well as the red stain on the back of his tank top. "You are bleeding. What happened?"

He pulled back the sheets and found a matching stain on the bed. Something silver jutted through a hole in the sheet. "A freaking spring from this bed stabbed me in the back, apparently."

"Ouch. Let me see if there are any first aid supplies in the medicine cabinet." Ainsley slid off the bed and went to the bathroom. Inside the cabinet above the sink, she found a mini first aid kit. Carrying it back to the room, she gestured for him to join her on the bed. "Come here. I'll try my best to patch you up."

"Thanks." He stood and removed his shirt.

His muscular chest came into view, and her mouth watered. His chiseled physique revealed his dedication to healthy eating and exercise, and he exuded a physical strength that captivated her. She imagined what it would be like to have him lift her into those strong arms, press her back against the nearest wall and make love to her until she lost her senses. Her naughty thoughts made her pulse quicken, so she did her best to push them away and focus on the task at hand.

As he sat on the bed, with his back to her, the sight of his wound dragged her back from fantasy to reality. A small, jagged gouge, about an inch long, lay just beneath his right shoulder blade. "Yikes."

"It hurts like hell." He groaned. "I knew the bed was a little lumpy, but I didn't know it was this serious."

She searched through the first aid kit and found an iodine wipe. Tearing open the foil packet, she applied the iodine to his wound as gently as she could.

He winced but otherwise kept his composure.

She dumped out the kit on the bed, separating the contents to find the ones she wanted. "I've cleaned it up. Now I'm gonna put some gauze and tape on it." Hoping to add a little humor to the situation, she added, "I'm sure Mary wouldn't want you ruining any more of her bed linens."

He chuckled. "I'm over here in pain and you're making it about Mary? Why do I put up with you?" His voice was tinged with mirth.

Working to tear off a small piece of medical tape, she placed it along the edge of the gauze square. "Face it, you need me. I keep you balanced." With the makeshift bandage secured, she patted it once more. "There. I'm done."

He turned to face her. "Thanks. And you're right, you do keep me balanced."

She winked. "I'm glad you can acknowledge the truth of things."

He straightened, looking her in the eye. "This little disaster means we need to revisit this whole 'one bed' thing."

She sucked in her lower lip. "I don't really want to sleep in the chair, and you aren't going to fit in the chair."

"I'm not about to be the one who makes the decision here, because above all else I want to make sure you feel comfortable."

She contemplated his words. She trusted him—that wasn't an issue. And she couldn't say parts of her weren't intrigued by the idea of sleeping in the same bed with him. "Let's just both sleep in the bed. Like you said, we're both mature adults, right?"

He watched her intently. "Right."

"And I'm too tired to be a troublemaker right now anyway." She yawned again. "Just pick a side and stay there, and I'll do the same. It'll be fine, right?"

"Yeah, yeah. It's no big deal."

She swallowed. He wasn't a creeper; he could keep to his side of the bed. What she'd be thinking about while he kept his distance from her...well, that was another matter entirely.

Once she was under the covers, leaving a wide berth between them, she whispered, "Good night, Gage."

"Good night."

She reached to the nightstand and switched off the lamp.

Eight

Ainsley awoke Tuesday morning feeling groggy and out of sorts. Blinking her eyes a few times as she came to full awareness, she shifted a bit then stopped as she realized where she was.

In the inn. In the bed. With Gage. And that would have been awkward enough...but she was also lying across his chest.

She turned her head slowly, her eyes widening as his chest hairs ticked her cheek. He was splayed out on his back, one hand behind his head and the other hand stroking her hair.

She squeezed her eyes shut, hoping she was dreaming.

But when she opened them again, the predicament remained.

Shit.

He stirred, and a moment later, his eyes popped open. "Good morning."

"Yeah, uh, good morning." She swallowed.

"Don't you look cozy?" He winked, fingers still entwined in her curls.

She jerked away from him. "Oh. I'm...so sorry. I must have been doing a lot of moving around. I sleep kinda wild."

He waved her off. "No need to apologize. It's not a problem."

She watched the expression playing over his face and thought she saw a hint of mischief in his eyes. Choosing not to dwell on it, she scooted away and got out of bed.

She found her bag kicked beneath the chair where she'd left it and pulled out the black three-quarter-sleeve tunic and charcoal-gray leggings she'd packed, along with underclothes.

Watching her from the bed, he asked, "You brought a change of clothes on a day trip?"

She nodded. "I always bring a change of clothes. I'm a klutz, and it's pretty likely I'm gonna spill something on myself, so I try to be prepared."

He chuckled. "If only I thought like you."

She grinned. "I'm one of a kind. The world couldn't handle another person who thought like me."

Tucking the clothes under her arm, she went to the bathroom and closed the door behind her.

Fresh from the shower, she emerged twenty or so minutes later to find Gage up and sitting in one of the armchairs, checking his voice mail. He had put his sleeveless undershirt back on, and she couldn't help dragging her gaze over his powerful biceps.

She passed him, going to the window to look outside. The skies were still gray, and the rain was coming down in buckets, but at least the hail seemed to have stopped. "After breakfast I'm going to head into town and see what stores are open."

He looked up from his phone. "In this weather? What, getting dinner yesterday wasn't enough of an adventure?"

She chuckled. "If I can find a clothing store, I can grab you a change of clothes." She grabbed her purse. "You're a thirty-eight waist and a nineteen shirt collar, right?"

"Right." A ghost of a smile crossed over his face. "Nothing too brightly colored, please."

Headed for the door, she tossed back, "I know you better than that, boss man. Come on downstairs. I can smell coffee."

After a delicious breakfast, Ainsley walked to the front desk, while Gage headed for the computer. Turning down the umbrella at the desk in favor of keeping her hands free, she donned a plastic poncho and left the inn. The short walk to town took her past groves of tall conifers encased in kudzu before the grass gave way to the concrete sidewalk and the forest to buildings of varying heights and sizes.

Looking down the road, she was again struck by the picturesque charm of Summer Village. Having lived in Atlanta her entire life, she couldn't imagine living in a place so small, without most of the amenities she'd become accustomed to. Still, there was something refreshing about the one- and two-story buildings, the hand-painted signs on businesses, and the old-fashioned feel the town evoked.

A short search led her to Kramer and Sons, a two-story menswear store. Once inside, she greeted the shopkeepers as she shook off her drenched poncho and left it by the door.

"I'm Ted, and this is my son, Teddy." The man, wearing a pair of khakis and a red polo, had a pair of copper-rimmed reading glasses perched atop his graying head.

"Nice to meet you both." She smiled. "I'm Ainsley."

Teddy, who was dressed identically to his father except that his polo was blue, asked, "What can I help you find, Miss Ainsley?"

She put in a request for Gage's size in shirts and slacks, and twenty minutes later, she left with a bag containing a pair of black slacks and a hunter green button-down. As she stepped outside, she stopped short, realizing he'd probably need boxers as well. *Good thing I've got the corporate credit card and a can-do spirit.* She chuckled as she went back inside.

She thought back to that morning, when she'd awakened sprawled across his chest, her eyes just inches away from the waistband of his boxers. She sucked her bottom lip into her mouth at the memory, then let herself follow that thread for just a minute before she shook it off.

She left the store a short while later with her purchases. The rain continued crashing down, but since she was soaked anyway, she decided instead of heading straight back to the inn, she'd look around. A few other rain-soaked people passed her on the sidewalk, and every one of them took the time to wave or say hello.

When the wind started blowing the rain sideways, she quickly ducked into the doorway of a small, one-story brick structure. *Glow Apothecary.* The window display included plenty of artfully arranged miniature Mason jars filled with all kinds of goodies for the hair, skin and body.

She entered the shop to the sound of the tinkling bell above the door.

A tall, slender Black woman with a glorious Afro waved at her from behind the counter. She wore a white top and matching slacks with a black apron over her clothes. "Come in, come in. Get out of this terrible weather. Welcome to my shop."

"Hi. I'm Ainsley." She removed her wet poncho before approaching the counter and set her bag down. "Nice place."

"Thanks for the compliment. I'm Candace, by the way." She stuck out her hand.

Ainsley shook it. "Is it okay if I leave my bag with you while I take a look around?"

"Sure thing."

She started walking the aisles, taking in the shelves lined with artfully arranged jars, bottles and tins. She unscrewed the lid off a small jar of grapefruit body scrub and inhaled deeply. She sighed as the invigorating scent of tart citrus flooded her nostrils. "This smells amazing, Candace."

"Thanks." She walked over to where Ainsley stood. "The citrus line is actually our most popular."

"How do you get it to smell like that? I feel like I just cut into a red grapefruit." She inhaled again and smiled. "I can almost taste it."

"Actually, I make all these products myself, with a little help from two of my cousins. We zest grapefruits, dry the little shreds of the rind and add them to the mixture. That increases the scent and adds to the exfoliating power."

"Wow." She couldn't help being impressed with Candace's artistry. As the conversation continued, she noticed the way Candace's face lit up as she spoke about her products. It occurred to her that her job as Gage's assistant didn't inspire anywhere near that level of excitement.

She belonged in human resources, where she could really use her skills to help everyone who worked for 404. That was where she truly felt her life's work lay.

While Candace chattered on about her lemon verbena body butter, Ainsley's eyes widened as the realization of something hit her.

It wasn't passion for her job that had kept her in the same position for five years.

It was passion for her *boss*.

She swallowed. After last night, when she'd lay over his body in her sleep as if it were the natural thing to do, she didn't think she could go back to pretending the attraction didn't exist.

Gage stood by the window, looking outside. The almost-black skies and torrential rain were starting to affect his mood in a major way, and he didn't think being in the room alone was helping matters any.

Summer Village seems like a nice enough place, but we've got to get the hell out of here.

Grabbing his cell phone, he called Max, praying she was somewhere near enough to civilization that she could get a signal.

She picked up on the third ring. "Morning, Gage. Before you ask, no, nothing has changed since you called me two hours ago."

"Damn. I'm just trapped in the inn with this terrible weather and no Wi-Fi. I'm going crazy." He sighed. "Where are you?"

"I'm in town at a little coffee shop. Mr. Delmar gave me a ride."

"What's going on with the plane, Max? Please tell me we can get back in the air today."

"That's not likely."

He groaned. "Why? It's not a mechanical problem, right?"

"No, not at all." Max chuckled. "It's a brand-new plane, remember? This is just an issue of fueling her up."

Gage ran a hand over his head. "Let me guess. Jet fuel isn't easy to come by way out here, is it?"

"Ding, ding, ding." She paused. "I'm actually gonna have to go to this tiny little airport up in Arkansas to get her refueled."

"If you can fly there then why can't we just load up, stop in for a fill-up and head to Cali? I need to get this equipment before Harcroft resells it."

"That's the plan, but we can't do it today. Visibility is less than ten percent, and unless this next line of storms moves really quickly, we're grounded for probably another eighteen hours. I'm so sorry, Gage. Even I can't fight Mother Nature."

His brow creased. "Did you say the next line of storms? Another one is coming?"

"Yes. It's all over the news. This line is just as strong as the last one but is moving a little slower. It's supposed to hit within the next two hours and last the rest of the day. We can't even get through it to fly above it."

"Shit." A curse was all he had at the moment.

"Listen, will you let me know as soon as we're clear to leave?"

"Sure thing."

After he ended the call, he checked the time. It was a good two or more hours since Ainsley had left. Curiosity about what she was up to had started to get the better of him. *What's she doing out there? It's been a while.*

The thought of looking for her crossed his mind, but he dismissed it. After all, she was an adult, and not his responsibility. If she got into some kind of trouble, she could handle it on her own. He'd always known Ainsley to be a very capable person.

His stomach growled loudly. He'd eaten a huge breakfast, but since it was nearly lunchtime, he was hungry again. *Looks like I'm going out.*

He went to the bathroom and got cleaned up. Then he got his slacks from the back of the chair where he'd draped them, shaking out the rumples before slipping them on. Once he was fully dressed, he got a rain poncho from Mary and ventured out of the inn.

The air was thick with humidity and held a slight chill. The rain hitting his face felt like being splashed with a cold beverage, so he walked quickly toward the town's Main Street.

When he came across the coffee shop, he went inside. Glancing around the interior for Max, he realized he must have missed her. The only other person inside was the barista behind the counter. "Hi. Can

I have an almond-milk latte with stevia and sugar-free hazelnut?"

The barista smiled but looked slightly confused. "I can make you a latte, sir, but we don't have sugar-free syrups. Or almond milk. Or what was that other thing?"

"Stevia. It's a sweetener."

The barista shrugged. "Sorry. We do have the stuff in the pink packets if you want that instead."

The idea of the pink stuff in his coffee was an immediate turnoff, so he just shook his head. "Never mind. I think I'll just grab lunch instead."

He left the coffee shop and, dodging the rain as much as possible, ran across the street to the Blue Rose Diner. He assumed it was the same place from yesterday, because he doubted a town this small had very many restaurants.

When he stepped inside, he found Ainsley at the counter chatting, her back to him. She clutched a paper shopping bag with twine handles in one hand. The shapely outline of her hips and thighs in the close-fitting tunic and leggings made his pulse quicken.

She turned around, her smile brightening his mood. "Oh, hey, Gage. Leave your poncho next to mine at the door, then come on and meet Rose and Bud."

He couldn't help chuckling. "Wow. Those your real names?"

"My name's Buford. Bud's a nickname." The man

in the apron looked less than amused. "But Rose is my wife's given name."

"Sorry." He swallowed, sensing he'd offended Bud. "I wasn't poking fun." And he wasn't. "I've just never encountered a couple with such complimentary names."

"Whatever you say." Bud moved away from the counter and went to the flat-top grill.

Rose interjected, "Don't mind my husband—he's saltier than brine at times. Welcome to the Blue Rose. What can I get you?"

"I'm going to confer with Ainsley before I decide," Gage answered, throwing Ainsley a grin.

Ainsley shook her head. "Really?"

"Absolutely." They stepped away from the counter, and he leaned close to her ear. "Do you want to eat here? I'm in no hurry to get back out in the rain."

"Sounds good." She paused, held up the shopping bag. "I managed to snag you a shirt and slacks."

He took the bag from her and glanced inside at the neatly folded—and dry—clothes. "Ainsley, you're a lifesaver."

She grinned. "I do my best." She tapped her chin, looking toward the menu board. "That bacon cheeseburger was awesome, but I feel like I should try something else. What are you gonna get?"

He shrugged. "Probably the same thing you brought me yesterday. I don't know if much else on the menu will work with my diet."

"True." She squinted. "Hmm. I think I'll try the

chicken club this time. Can't go wrong with bacon and cheese, right?" She winked.

He shook his head. "I think I hear your arteries crying."

"Nope. That's the sound of my stomach singing in anticipation." Laughing, she left him standing there as she walked back toward the counter to order.

Watching her hips sway, he couldn't help smiling. He'd been so frustrated since they landed in Summer Village because he hated having his plans altered. Aside from that, there was a lot at stake here for the company. But when he looked at her, heard her witty repartee and the tinkling of her laughter, everything suddenly seemed right.

She's really something special.

And I want her. Not just as my assistant, but as my woman.

Nine

Back at the counter, Ainsley placed her order. When she finished, Gage stepped up. "We'll be on the same ticket."

Ainsley balked. "You don't have to do that."

"I know, but I insist." Gage turned his attention back to Rose. "Let me have your grilled chicken salad, no dairy, no carbs and fat-free dressing on the side, please. And I'll be drinking water."

"No problem, honey." Rose typed in the order.

As he took out his wallet to pay, Bud appeared behind his wife again. "You know, the little lady ordered the exact same thing yesterday. Said it was for her boss."

Gage nodded. "Yeah, that's me."

Bud snickered. "I thought for sure she worked for another woman. But I see you're just a pampered city-boy type instead." He looked him up and down with thinly veiled disdain.

Gage's jaw tightened, and Ainsley noticed the irritation clouding his face. She'd never understood the pissing contests men seemed to love having with each other. *Bud doesn't know Gage from a can of paint. He's in no position to be passing judgment on him.*

"Bud!" Rose spun on him. "Get back to your grill and keep your smart mouth shut before I box your ears!" Turning back to them, she gave them foam cups with the diner's logo printed on them.

Bud backed up a step. "Now, Rose, I was just—"

"You were just what? Insulting a paying customer?" Ainsley knew her tone was sharp, but she thought it appropriate for the situation. "I like you, Bud. You're a straight shooter, and I can respect that. But I'm telling you right now, nobody talks trash about my boss but me."

A perturbed-looking Gage eyed Ainsley. "Say what now?"

"Don't worry. Just enough trash talk to keep you humble." She nodded.

He shook his head but still let a smile tilt his full lips.

Bud threw up his hands. "I'm going back to my kitchen."

After they filled their cups at the drink machine,

Gage walked behind Ainsley, following her to the booth she chose near the back. Once they were seated across from each other, she asked, "What made you decide to leave the room?"

I missed you. He didn't know how that would go over if he said it aloud. "Stir-crazy, I guess. It's crappy weather, but it was still high time I got out of there."

"Fair enough." She sipped her soda through the striped straw.

"Listen. I just wanted to say thanks for coming to my defense."

She waved him off. "It's nothing."

"Still. I appreciate you speaking on my behalf." He looked into her eyes. "I know you didn't have to do that."

"You're welcome." She let her gaze drop, a bit overwhelmed by the intensity in his eyes.

"You do so much that makes things easier for me, and I really haven't been as appreciative as I should have. That's going to change from now on."

"Wow, Gage." She stirred her drink around a few times, needing the distraction. "I don't know what to say."

"You don't have to say anything. I'm going to show you how much you mean to me."

She looked up from her cup and found him watching her. There was something in his eyes this time, something quite different. He'd made some strong declarations, and at first, she'd thought he was talking about work. Now it seemed to go much deeper than that.

Could this be it? Could this be the moment he realized how much she wanted to be with him, that they were meant for each other? After so many years of pining for him, it all seemed too much to hope for.

Rose appeared next to the table with the bright red trays holding their food. "You two enjoy."

After she walked away, Ainsley dug into her sandwich. She needed time to analyze and process what was happening right now. Her heart was on the line here, and she didn't want to risk misreading anything and making a dumb mistake that would leave her brokenhearted and looking foolish.

"Any word from Max on when we can leave?" She needed to change the subject before things got any more intense.

"Eager to get home, huh?" He blessed her with a megawatt smile.

"Honestly, yes. I miss Cooper. And besides that, I'm worried he may be eating my neighbors out of house and home." She chuckled, though she'd only been half joking. Her son could put away food like a human garbage disposal.

"Max is hoping we can get off the ground tomorrow. There's a second wave to the storms, and she said visibility is almost nonexistent for now." He forked up some of his salad.

She sighed. "I'm sorry, Gage. I know how you

like keeping to a tight schedule, so I know this little unexpected detour must be driving you bonkers."

He chewed, looking thoughtful, then swallowed. "You know what? It was bugging me. But I'm beginning to embrace what's happening."

She frowned, confused. *That doesn't sound like the regimented man I've known for all this time.* "Why's that?"

"For two reasons. One, we have to make safety our absolute first priority. If it's not safe to fly, then we need to stay put."

"I agree. What's the other reason?" She put a fry in her mouth.

"You. I couldn't ask for better company. And even though we aren't supposed to be here, I'm enjoying spending time with you, away from the office."

Her eyes widened, and she had to snatch up her cup and quickly wash the wayward fry down before she succumbed to a coughing fit.

"You okay?" He stood up.

"I'm fine, I'm fine." She took a deep breath, then one more sip of soda. "Just…uh…a little surprised to hear you talking like this."

"I have to admit, I didn't intend on saying all that out loud." He sat back down. "But I'm glad I did. It's high time we're honest with each other about how we feel."

She gave him a sidelong glance. "We? Oh, you speak French now?"

"Don't try to play me like that. You know what I'm talking about."

"I just think it's mighty cocky of you to say it that way. As if you're so sure I have feelings for you. You ain't all that, Gage Woodson." She couldn't resist teasing him some more. Not only did it amuse her, but it helped to defuse some of the rising romantic tension she sensed between them.

He simply shook his head. "Nice try. But you can't deny it, Ainsley. I feel it, you feel it. It's been there for a long, long time."

She looked out the window, knowing that if she made eye contact with him, it was over for her.

They finished their food, and she avoided his gaze the entire time. When she got up to discard their trash, he called after her.

"You're going to have to look at me sometime, Ainsley."

It was all she could do to get the emptied trays into the slot on top of the trash can. As she walked back to the table, he stepped in front of her. With a gentle hand beneath her chin, he tilted her head, effectively forcing her to look up.

"What do you need, Ainsley? Is there something you want?"

Oh, you have no idea. "There's some pricey body scrub at the apothecary I had my eye on."

"Take me there, and it's yours." He held her gaze for a moment, then let his hand fall away.

Walking with him out of the diner, she couldn't help noticing the knowing looks on Rose and Bud's faces.

Despite being back outside in the dreary weather, Gage felt his mood lighten considerably because now, Ainsley walked by his side. Their meal together had turned into something of a confessional for him. He typically avoided any conversations about emotions and feelings, and he still wasn't quite sure what had come over him. All he knew was that he cared about Ainsley, and that he wanted a much deeper connection with her than just their working relationship.

The ball was in her court, though. What he wanted in no way superseded her autonomy. His mother, Addison, had raised all her children as womanists, and those teachings were deeply ingrained in his mind. He'd never disrespect Ainsley or do anything to make her feel uncomfortable. So now that the truth was out, he'd simply have to follow her cues, whatever that might lead to.

He watched her as she walked beside him. Even in the rain-dappled poncho and sensible outfit, she radiated beauty. Her gaze rested on the scenery as they passed, and he wondered if she were avoiding his eyes again. He smiled. Suddenly, his effervescent assistant had become somewhat shy, a quality he'd never known her to exhibit before.

"Here's the place." She grasped the door handle at Glow Apothecary.

"Allow me." He reached to open the door, and

their hands grazed momentarily, sending a charge of magic up his arm. He held open the door for her to walk in, then followed her inside.

The interior was small, but the setup showed creative use of the space. The displays were both aesthetic and practical, and the whole place smelled like warm sugar cookies. It was, hands down, the most inviting place in Summer Village. He heard a familiar beat, playing softly from a hidden speaker. Listening intently, he tilted his head and stood near the middle of the store until he identified the song. "'Good Lovin'? Classic Atlanta hip-hop. That song doesn't get enough love."

"Thanks. Not everyone around here appreciates my taste in music." The Black woman behind the counter, who introduced herself as Candace, offered a bright grin before turning her attention to Ainsley. "Good to see you back so soon!" It was obvious she and Ainsley had a certain rapport. He could feel himself smiling. There was something about watching Black women chatting, laughing and enjoying each other's company that always warmed his heart. While he was eager to spoil Ainsley a little, he hung back and let them talk.

After a few minutes, Ainsley turned his way. "So, the stuff I wanted is over here."

Candace's expression brightened. "Oh, honey. You didn't tell me earlier you were here on a little romantic getaway." She winked.

Ainsley's wide-eyed expression, a mixture of embarrassment and humor, was priceless. She swallowed visibly but didn't say anything.

Under normal circumstances, he would have corrected Candace. But considering all he'd said a short time ago, he simply slipped his arm around Ainsley's shoulders and said, "Show me what you want."

"I'll leave you two to your shopping. Let me know if you need any help." A still-grinning Candace returned to her post behind the counter.

Ainsley led him to a section where baskets of wax fruit adorned the displays and showed him Glow's grapefruit and shea collection. Grabbing a tin of body scrub from the shelf, she twisted off the cap and held it up to his nose. "You have to smell this. It's amazing."

He inhaled, and the fresh, bright aroma washed over him. "Wow. That does smell good."

"I know, right?" She screwed the lid back on. "They have so much good stuff in this scent." She gestured to the shelf as she spoke. "There's handmade soap, body butter..."

She kept listing products, but most of it went underwater as he fixated on the phrase *handmade soap*. His mind flashed to an image of her, reclining in the old claw-foot tub in their room, gliding a soapy cloth over her beautiful dark skin as steam rose around her like a fog.

The proprietor's voice cut into his fantasy. "If you buy the collection, you get a free Glow Apothecary silk robe."

They both turned toward the counter.

Candace chuckled. "Just letting y'all know."

He returned his attention to Ainsley. "Can't knock the hustle, right?"

"Yeah, right." She giggled. "But I don't expect you to buy me all of this stuff."

"I'm going to buy it all." He kept his gaze fixed on her.

Her eyes widened again. "But Gage. That's almost…"

"I'm in operations. I'm good at math, and I know how much it's gonna cost." He started gathering the various jars and bottles of each product. "It's still not a bad deal. Remember, you're getting a free robe."

She blinked. "Wait. You can't…"

"Can't what? I'm going to buy this for you, Ainsley. When's the last time you bought something for yourself anyway?"

She looked thoughtful for a long moment. "It's been forever since I brought something this frivolous. Most of my money either goes to Cooper's basic needs, his extracurricular activities or his college fund. The rest is eaten up on living expenses."

"Let me ask you something." He held the items from the collection in the crook of his arm. "Is this bath stuff gonna make you feel relaxed and calm?"

She nodded.

"Then don't call it frivolous." He started walking toward the counter. "Candace, can you total this up for us? And let her pick out her free robe."

"Gladly." Candace took the items and began ringing them into the register. After that, she gestured to the rainbow of silk robes hanging on the wall behind her. "What color and size, sweetie?"

"Let me get the lavender one. Size large." Ainsley still looked a bit taken aback by what was happening, but at least she seemed to understand now that he wasn't going to be dissuaded from making the purchase.

"Sure thing." Candace added a new, plastic-wrapped robe to the bag and quoted a total to Gage. He paid with his credit card, and soon they were on their way again, each carrying shopping bags. She was quiet for the rest of the walk, and he didn't press her since she seemed to be thinking about something.

They arrived at the inn thoroughly damp, and he could feel the chill starting to get to him as he stepped up on the porch.

They stopped there, neither of them reaching for the door.

"Thank you, Gage." Her voice was soft.

Facing her, he stroked her jawline. "You're welcome." Tilting her chin, he asked, "Can I kiss you?" Without waiting for a response, he pressed his lips against hers as the rain battered the roof.

Ten

Upstairs in their room, Ainsley felt her cheeks warm as Gage watched her carry her bag of body products to the bathroom door. The afternoon was now turning darker as more storm clouds rolled in. She'd done a lot of walking today. *Better to take care of it now than be sore tomorrow.* "I think I'm going to take a hot bath."

"Be my guest." He smiled at her as she shut the bathroom door behind her.

The bathroom, with its pink, ivy-print wallpaper, pink toilet and pedestal sink, and pictures of roses on the wall, reflected a taste in home decor she certainly didn't share. She did, however, approve of the deep, welcoming-looking bathtub that centered the space. It was painted the same shade of pink as the other fixtures, but the overall shape and design of the tub made it the showpiece of the room. A short-legged wooden stool had been placed next to the tub.

While she unloaded the bag onto the small wall shelf next to the sink, she reflected on the kiss they'd just shared on the front porch of the inn. Of all the things she'd thought might happen today, getting kissed by her boss hadn't even been in the realm of possibility. Now, she knew that nothing would ever be the same between them. Whether that was a good or a bad thing remained to be seen.

She moved over to the old claw-foot tub. It took some maneuvering to get the hot water handle to turn, but when she finally did, a torrent of water rushed forth, so loud it almost drowned out the sounds of the falling rain. Passing her hand under the water, she waited for it to get nice and hot before inserting the rubber stopper into the drain. As the tub began to fill, she unscrewed the lid to the bubbling bath salts and used the small enclosed scooper to add some to the water. The sweet, fresh aroma of citrus filled the room, and she sighed.

There are so many things going through my head. In a way, I don't know how I should feel.

But right now, with the slight tingle in her lips and the memory of Gage's kiss lingering in her mind, she felt pretty damn good about it. She'd carried this torch for him for five years, watching and waiting for any sign that he felt the same way. There had been glimmers of hope along the way, but no proof as solid as his behavior today.

Apparently, my patience has finally paid off. While the tub filled, she stripped off her clothes, folding the items neatly and placing them on the stool with her phone on top. When she shut off the water, the room was filled with steam, just the way she liked it when she decided to have a good soak. With a soft washcloth and her soap in hand, she stepped into the tub.

A sigh of pleasure escaped her lips as the hot water enveloped her. The tub was deep enough that the water came up to her shoulder blades, and she could feel the tension in her muscles melting away on the spot. This little pit stop in Louisiana hadn't been on the agenda when they'd left Atlanta, but this steamy bath, and the peace and quiet surrounding her, were almost enough to make this little detour worth the trouble.

There was a tub in her master bathroom back home. Though it wasn't as nice as this one, she tried to use it as often as she could. A lot of factors had to align for that to happen—the plumbing and water pressure had to cooperate, Cooper had to be occupied or out of the house, and she had to be alert enough that she didn't fear falling asleep while she was in there.

She wondered what her son was up to, and if he were getting on Bebe's nerves. Reaching for her phone, she texted her neighbor to check in on him. A response came in a few seconds later.

Cooper is fine. Fate has given you a break. Enjoy it.

She chuckled. Old straight-talking Bebe. She'd been a lifeline to her, especially since her cousin and former roommate Eden had moved out and gotten married.

She used her music subscription service to start up a soft contemporary jazz station, then set the phone aside. Since she stayed busy with Cooper, tied up with work or household stuff, tired, or all of the above most of the time, she was accustomed to taking quick showers most days. A bath seemed like decadence, a rare luxury. She scooted down until the water rose up to her neck, determined to enjoy this to the fullest.

With the relaxing music filling the room, she let her eyes close and her mind wander. A few random ideations passed through, but they were soon replaced by her thoughts of Gage. What they'd shared today…she couldn't get the memory of his kiss out of her head. And she didn't want to.

What's going to happen between us now? Are we gonna be an item? Will things get super weird at work? She couldn't answer any of those questions. All she knew was that she'd been enamored with him since the first time she laid eyes on him, and whatever the consequences might be, she just couldn't pass up this chance to find out what could develop between them.

She touched her lips, sending a few droplets of water running down her chin. Kissing him, after wanting to for so long, had felt like something special. The charge that went through her body effectively changed her, removing any notion that they could remain strictly colleagues. And honestly, she felt like that had been Gage's intent. A lot could be communicated through a kiss, and that kiss seemed to say, "I want you."

She sucked in her bottom lip, realizing that while she soaked, he was right outside the door. She hadn't heard him moving around and assumed he was keeping quiet for her benefit.

Here they were, in this room in the middle of nowhere, where they barely knew a soul. In this room with just one bed. She wasn't terribly religious, but she did believe that the universe put us in the place we were meant to be, at the time we were meant to be there. This little side trip was almost a cosmic setup, an insistence that they explore their attractions.

She imagined him in the room with her. In her mind's eye, she saw him approach the tub, his shirtless torso revealing his hard-earned strength. Kneeling beside the tub, he took the cloth from her trembling hand and soaped it. He mouthed the words, *Want me to wash your back?* It was all she could do to nod. He smiled, then began sliding the sudsy cloth over her skin...

A sudden thud snapped her back to reality. She sat up, water sloshing around her, and looked for the source of the sound. Seeing that her phone had slipped off the stool onto the floor, she blew out a breath. Cooper had texted her a good-night message, and the vibration must have sent the device crashing to the floor. The water was starting to cool, so she picked up the soap and bathed, all the while daydreaming it was Gage moving the cloth.

Once she was clean, she drained the water. Using some of the body butter from the apothecary, she moisturized her skin before slipping into her new robe. Gathering everything back into the shopping bag, including her clothes and phone, she gripped the handle of the bathroom door.

Gage was sitting on the bed when Ainsley walked out of the bathroom, clad in the silken robe they'd purchased earlier. He swallowed, his mouth watering as he surmised her nudity beneath.

The television was still on, a remnant of his attempt to stop thinking about her bathing. He'd done his best to focus on the cable news station, but the scent of her bath products and steam wafting from the bathroom had completely killed his interest in anything else but her.

With the shopping bag in hand and the bundle of her clothes tucked beneath her arm, she walked past him and deposited everything beside the chair she'd been favoring since they arrived. Turning back his way, she watched him for a moment. "Gage? Are you okay?"

"I'm fine," he insisted, his tone gruffer than he'd meant it to be.

"Just making sure, because you look like you swallowed a bug."

He laughed. She always knew when to crack a corny joke. She wasn't a comedian per se, but she had excellent comedic timing. "Damn, Ainsley."

She shrugged, feigning innocence. "What? I mean if you swallowed a foreign object, you may need medical intervention."

His laughter only increased as she went on joking about this supposed bug he'd swallowed. Every time he stopped laughing for a minute, he'd look at her, see that deadpan expression, and he'd start up all over again.

Soon she broke and started laughing along with him.

When he finally calmed down and got his breath, he said, "Thanks. I needed that laugh." It had given him the mental space to think more clearly about his feelings.

"I know you did." She gave his hand a small squeeze. "My particular brand of goofy has its benefits."

Something came over him in that moment, and he grasped her hand a little tighter. "Did you…enjoy your bath?"

She sucked in her bottom lip. "I did. Thanks again for all the fancy bath stuff."

"You're welcome." He gazed into the shimmering depths of her brown eyes. "It's the least I could do, considering everything you do for me."

"Oh, come on. Not that again." She shrugged, her gaze dropping as if she were suddenly becoming shy. "I always try to be the best assistant I can."

"You have to know by now that you're so much more than an assistant to me, Ainsley." He tugged her a bit closer to him and used his fingertip to trace slow circles over her jawline. "Or did I not make that clear earlier when I kissed you?"

She stared up at him, her eyes wide.

"Thank you, Ainsley, for everything you do that makes my life better."

She swallowed, nodded. "You…uh…you're welcome."

There was silence between them for a few long seconds.

Then he spoke. If he didn't lay his cards out now, who knew when he'd get another chance?

But before he could open his mouth, she spoke.

"This may be off base, and please tell me if it is, but…" She touched his arm, slowly moving her hand until it was over his heart. "I think we should… I mean…do you want to just…you know…do it?"

His brow hitched, his heart pounding. "I need you to be specific."

"Make love."

"Is that what you want?" He picked up her hand from his chest, kissed it.

Her answering sigh was followed by, "Oh yes."

"Absolutely." He led her by the hand to the armchair. Taking a seat, he pulled her into his lap. A moment later, she leaned in for his kiss.

He groaned as their lips met, tasting the remnants of her lip gloss. Her lips were soft, yielding, intoxicating. Holding her body close to his, he licked her lips and she opened to him, letting his tongue delve into the sweetness of her mouth.

She shifted in his lap, and he could feel her tugging at his shirt buttons as they continued to kiss. Breaking the contact, he unbuttoned his own shirt while holding her gaze.

Her tongue darted out, sliding across the fullness of her bottom lip. "I want you so bad." The words were barely a whisper, a quiet declaration in the darkness-shrouded room.

"Don't worry. You got me." He stood then, lifting her with him, and carried her the short distance to the bed.

There, he quickly stripped her of her robe. Leaving her briefly to grab the small packet of condoms he kept in his attaché case, he returned and tucked one beneath a pillow. Stripping down to his boxers, he joined her on the bed. Hearing her sigh when their bodies touched, he pulled her into his arms and began kissing her again.

With the rain falling from the cloud-shrouded sky,

and the dim light coming from the streetlamp outside, he moved his kisses slowly down her body. First, the sweet-swelling curve of her neck and shoulders. Then, he drew each dark nipple into his mouth, sucking and licking until she whimpered. He placed a series of leisurely kisses between the full globes of her breasts, down her stomach, until he settled his face between her thighs.

"Gage…"

Before she could utter another word, he'd placed her legs over his shoulders. Leaning into her mound, he buried his face there, his tongue finding her swollen bud right away. Circling it, teasing it, he listened to the sounds she made and observed the movements of her body to learn what pleased her. She was sweet, hot and flowing, her sex glistening from arousal. He found the pattern that made her moan and made her back arch, then kept that cadence as he slipped a finger inside her. When he crooked his finger gently, she screamed, and he could feel the wetness flowing down his hand in the darkness.

Satisfied that she'd gotten that first orgasm, he crawled up beside her for a kiss. She moaned into his mouth and suddenly gave him an insistent shove, rolling him onto his back. Straddling him, she asked, "Protection?"

He swallowed, getting the condom from where he'd put it and handing it to her. While he watched, she tore open the packet and held his gaze as she covered his hardness. It was one of the most erotic sights he'd ever seen. No sooner had she protected them than she positioned herself and lowered her body onto his.

He gasped as her tightness enveloped him, consuming his entire being. Her motions were skillful and slow as she rose and fell, softly purring with pleasure. The subtle bounce of her breasts enraptured him, and he reached up to touch them, palming and squeezing the firm globes. Then he slid his hands down and gripped her sides as she rode him, and his vision swam as pleasure made his eyes roll back in his head.

She was magnificent. Better than any lover before, and far above any fantasy his mind had ever created. The way her body moved, the way she gripped him so perfectly as if their bodies were made to fit together. The sounds she made with each roll of her hips. Nothing compared to her, to this moment and the fire spreading through his very soul.

"Oh shit." She whispered the words as her head lolled back, and she increased the pace of her ride.

He slid his hands over her sweat-dampened skin, cupping her ass in his hands. Moments later, she was coming, her inner muscles flexing around him.

He lost all control and growled as his own release tore through him. She collapsed on top of him, and he held her close, letting his heavy eyes drift closed.

Eleven

Ainsley awakened in the morning darkness to the feeling of Gage's lips brushing over the plane of her stomach. She shifted a bit, feeling the smile tipping her lips. "And just what are you doing down there, sir?"

"What do you think?" His reply was tinged with mischief as he continued to move his warm lips over her sensitive flesh.

The trembling set in again as his actions reminded her of their lovemaking, of the passion he'd awakened in her. A soft moan escaped her lips.

"That's the spirit." His voice had taken on a downright wicked edge, and she didn't fight him when he eased her thighs apart and slipped between them.

After he'd reduced her to screams again, she came back to herself and turned the tables on him. Getting him onto his back, she murmured, "Turnabout is fair play." A breath later, she took his dick into her mouth. She gave as good as she received, letting her desire show through in the way she worked her mouth over his hard flesh. Before long he was pushing her away. With a groan, he positioned her on her hands and knees, entering her from behind.

Later, she lay in his arms, feeling safer than she'd felt in years. Being with him like this all night, while new and somewhat unfamiliar, felt right. She had no idea what time it was, but as the colors of dawn began to splash across the sky, she lay there listening to him tell stories from his childhood. He'd never been one to disclose much about his personal life, so she let him talk.

She rested her back against the pile of pillows, with him lying on his back between her legs, staring up at the ceiling as he spoke. "I remember all kinds of shenanigans my siblings and I pulled when we were younger. It's a miracle our parents didn't put us in a box and ship us off to our family up in Jersey."

"That bad, huh?"

"Think about it. It was a literal house full of kids. Three boys and two girls. Nia, being the oldest, did her best to help wrangle the rest of us—I think that's why she's so serious. But a lot of the time, we still got into trouble."

She chuckled. "Tell me about it."

"For example, Teagan used to be obsessed with rabbits. I mean high-key obsessed. One time, when she and Miles were about three years old, she wandered off from our backyard following a bunny. It took two hours of searching before we found her, curled up asleep under a tree about a quarter-mile beyond the property line." He shook his head. "I think my mom got her first patch of gray hairs that day."

"Yikes." She cringed. "I know what that's like. I think most parents do. Cooper wandered off from me in the mall when he was about that age. I freaked out for ten minutes before I found him hiding behind one of those big planters near the food court. He was laughing so hard because he thought it was just another game of hide-and-seek. And there I was, crying and on the verge of a breakdown."

"Wow." He shook his head. "Then there was the time Blaine and I were roughhousing, and I ended up having to go to the hospital because I cracked my head on a door frame. I think I was like twelve or thirteen when that happened." He scratched his chin. "Or when Miles tripped over a cord and landed on a crossfader Dad had been setting up in the studio and shattered the damn thing."

"Crossfader. The thing on the soundboard?"

"Yep. Dad had to replace it, to the tune of thousands of dollars." He could still see the look on his father's face, a mixture of frustration and anger. "He barred all the kids from the studio for like a year, and made Miles work off the cost of the equipment by doing odd jobs around the house."

"Y'all certainly did cause your parents a lot of grief, huh?" She laughed. "But there have to be some good memories, too, right?"

"Oh sure. For us, as the kids, there are plenty of those. Sleepovers. Birthday parties. Cookouts. Family vacations." He smiled, but it didn't quite reach his eyes. "I don't think my parents have as many happy memories, though."

She frowned. "What makes you say that?"

"Raising us cost them so much. Not just in money, but in time. In the ability to do the things they wanted to do for themselves. In disappointment and frustration." The smile faded away. "That's what parenting is. A long road paved with sacrifices and unpaid labor."

She didn't know how to respond to that, because there was definitely some truth in what he'd said. She'd fallen into bed many a night both physically and emotionally drained by mothering. She'd cried over missed opportunities and gatherings she couldn't attend because she didn't have a sitter. Despite it all, though, she couldn't imagine her life without her son.

"I just don't think I'm cut out for fatherhood, you know?" He sighed. "Maybe I'm too selfish. But I just can't see myself sacrificing on that level for so many years. It just seems like too much."

She swallowed. *So that's his view of parenting?*

That it's this horrible slog through life, where your child acts as a weight dragging you down into the abyss? She'd dated a few men who expressed doubts or downright refused to engage with the idea of raising a child. Yet she'd never encountered someone who seemed to genuinely disdain children. Looking back on his interaction with the middle schoolers who had visited the office, and some of the remarks she'd heard him make in passing over the past five years, she supposed she should have picked up on this attitude earlier.

His phone rang, bringing an end to the awkward silence between them. He glanced at the screen before answering it in a hushed tone. "Hello?"

She watched as he scrambled from the bed, hastily pulling on his pants and shirt. "I need to step out to take this," he whispered, his hand over the mic.

"Okay." A bit confused, she watched him slip from the room, shutting the door behind him.

What was that all about? She decided not to dwell on it, because even though they'd just slept together, she knew that didn't entitle her to know every single detail of his personal life. Grabbing the remote, she switched on the television to catch one of the national morning news shows.

While the anchor delivered a news story about the line of storms that had trapped them here in the first place finally beginning to move toward the coast, she sighed. *I should be listening to this, but I can't stop thinking about what Gage just said. He seemed to genuinely dislike the idea of raising a child.* But if they were to have any shot at a relationship, he'd have to be able to love and guide Cooper until he reached adulthood, and that was a nonnegotiable fact. She refused to be romantically involved with a man who couldn't tolerate her child, no matter how handsome that man might be.

She got up long enough to slip on her clothes, so he wouldn't think she'd be up for another round of lovemaking when he returned from his top-secret call. Then she sat down in her armchair, trying not to look at the rumpled bed.

"Good morning, Miles." Gage walked downstairs and into the breakfast room. The sunlight streaming through the windows gave the place a soft glow, and he felt thankful for a break in the weather. The air held the scent of bacon, and as he passed the counter where the food was laid out, he noted the scrambled eggs, English muffins and fresh fruit accompanying his favorite source of protein.

"Good morning yourself," Miles snapped.

"Somebody's grumpy." Spotting the coffee bar, he fixed himself a mug, nodding to a few others seated in the room before finding his own table. Settled into the chair, he said, "What's the matter? Woke up on the wrong side of a hookup?"

"Shut up, Gage." Miles yawned. "I'm only talking to you right now so Mom won't take me into the kickboxing ring."

"What's up?"

"Seriously, bruh? You were supposed to be back in town with the equipment two days ago! You didn't call anyone here to let them know there was a problem. And now you're surprised to hear from me?"

He chuckled. "I guess not. We had a little weather-related snafu."

"Well, that's nice to know. When you didn't come back Monday, we assumed it was just a delay. But yesterday, Mom got worried. So, she called Max and discovered you're in Louisiana, cold chillin'?"

"I wouldn't say that." He rubbed a hand over his face. "Listen. I'm sorry I didn't call. But I did check in with Harcroft to let them know we were delayed."

"Wonderful. Check in with them but just forget about your family." Miles didn't bother hiding the irritation in his voice. "Mom was worried."

"You already said that." *What you mean is you were worried.* Gage sighed, knowing his baby brother would never admit to being concerned for his safety. "Look, I know I should have called, and I already said I'm sorry. But the weather's improved, so hopefully, we can get in the air and out of Podunk today. So, can you chill?"

"Normally, I would absolutely be chill. But there have been some developments here while you've been enjoying the quaint scenery of an idyllic town in the Deep South, Gage."

He rolled his eyes. "Miles, what are you flapping your gums about now?"

"The Visionary had some kind of epiphany, a fit of artistic inspiration."

"That's great." That meant they could expect some stellar tracks from the album, the publicity from which could only draw even more high-profile clients to the studio to record.

"Yeah, but I'm not finished. Apparently, he sat down and wrote the lyrics for an entire album over the last few days. Yesterday, the producers got in contact with Teagan about coming in sooner to record his album. *Sooner.*" He emphasized the last word.

Gage felt his throat tighten. "How soon?"

"Friday."

"As in, two days from now?"

"Well, look at that. You *do* have a sense of time."

"Watch it, Miles."

"Whatever. You'd better get your asses back here with that equipment, quick, fast and in a hurry," Miles groused. "As head of finance, I don't even want to think about the kind of money we'd lose if The Visionary takes his album elsewhere to record."

Gage cringed. Even though Miles hadn't said it, he could tell that his brother still held some resentment against him for Tara's embezzlement. *This is my chance to help us make up that shortfall.* "Listen. I'm gonna do my best to get the equipment back there, ASAP."

"We really need you to come through on this,

Gage. So cut your little impromptu vacation short, please."

"I assure you, I'm not on vacation. As for enjoying this town, I'd say it's quite the opposite. The whole place is about the size of a postage stamp, and it lacks so many things. I've been called a city boy just because I enjoy certain conveniences. There isn't even wireless internet where we're staying."

"Where are you even staying there?" Miles's footsteps could be heard as he walked around. "I was curious, so I looked it up online, and there aren't any hotels near that place."

Gage shook his head. His brother had been nosy—under the guise of being "curious"—ever since they were kids. "We lucked out. Found a little bed-and-breakfast."

"And Max stayed on the plane. She told Mom that much." There was a pause. "Gage, how big is this bed-and-breakfast you're staying at?"

"Not very."

Another pause. "So…in this 'not very big' place… did you and Ainsley get separate rooms?"

He swallowed. "What kind of question is that?"

"Oh shit."

Gage frowned. "Miles, don't start with me."

"Y'all sharing a room." He stated it rather than asking. "Oh shit!"

"Damn, Miles. Can you relax?"

"No, I can't relax. Your voice went up half an

octave, and it always does that when you're hiding something. You definitely slept with her, and I—"

The call-waiting alert went off in his ear. Talk about saved by the bell. "I gotta go, Miles. Max is calling me."

"Yeah, whatever. But this conversation ain't over, bruh."

It gave him great pleasure to hang up on his brother and accept Max's call instead. "What's up, Max?"

"Hi, Gage. The weather's finally broken and visibility is crystal clear, so we can get out of here this morning. But just to be sure we can avoid any more weather, I'd like to be wheels up in an hour. Can you two make it back to the airstrip by then?"

"Yeah. We'll figure it out." No way was he about to stay here any longer than necessary, especially not with what he now knew about The Visionary. "See you soon."

Hanging up, he looked at the food and realized they hadn't had breakfast here yet. Draining his coffee, he pocketed his phone and jogged back upstairs to let Ainsley know of these new developments.

He found her in the chair, her attention focused on her tablet.

"Hey, Max says we can leave, but we need to get to the airstrip in an hour."

"Okay." She closed the cover over her tablet, got up, and started packing her bag. During this whole series of actions, she never once made eye contact with him.

He frowned. *What's the matter with her?* "The breakfast down there looks surprisingly good. Do you want to grab some on the way out?"

"Sure." Again, she spoke without looking in his direction. Unsure of what to make of her attitude, he went to gather his things so they could go.

With their bags in hand, they went downstairs and ate a silent meal together. Ainsley barely looked up from her plate. *What's with her? Does she not want to leave, or is it something else?*

At the desk, they had a brief chat with Mary, the innkeeper, and secured a ride to the airstrip with Hugh Delmar, the man who'd brought them to town on Monday.

They rode to entire way to the airstrip with only Hugh talking. While he chattered on about being relieved that the sun had finally returned to Summer Village, Ainsley stared out the window and Gage only nodded in response to Hugh's words. Her silence had soured his mood, and he didn't want to make things even worse by saying something wrong. Sure, he'd had some concern that making love to her might make their relationship awkward, but he certainly hadn't expected this.

The barn came into view. *At least we won't be so close to each other once we're back on the plane.*

Right now, she seemed to be pressing herself against Hugh to avoid touching thighs with him, and he just couldn't figure her out.

Twelve

Strapped into her seat on the plane, Ainsley sighed when Gage sat down in the seat next to her. While he buckled himself in, she focused on her tablet screen. She was less than a hundred pages from the end of the first book in the series she'd been reading, and she wanted to finish it before they landed in California. Aside from that, she had nothing to say to him right now.

"Aren't you glad to be leaving this one-horse town? Maybe now I can finally get a decent latte."

She leaned toward the window, hoping her body language would convey her disinterest. He'd spent all that time talking about how awful children were, and now he'd moved on to insulting an entire town and its residents. She would have told him to shut up, that the people there were perfectly nice and that not everyone felt the need to be so anal about their diet. But she didn't because that would involve talking to him.

He watched her for a moment, then slipped his arm around her shoulders. "After we get the equipment squared away, our next stop should be Starbucks. There's one not too far from Harcroft."

Her annoyance rumbled through her just like the plane's engine vibrating the floor beneath her feet. "Look, I really want to finish this book. Can you just...give me some space?"

"That's funny. You didn't seem to want any space last night."

Ugh. Is he really going to be that guy? The one who acts like sex with him is so life-changing you'll never be the same? She stared at him, wishing the heat in her glare could singe that smirk right off his face. "Gage, get away from me."

He looked as if he took offense, but he unbuckled his belt and did as she asked, moving his handsome, infuriating self and his case across the aisle. As they finally took off, she started reading her book again, determined that she would ignore his presence for the entirety of the flight.

After a quick refueling stop in Arkansas, the plane landed at Oakland International Airport around ten o'clock local time. As soon as they came to a stop, Ainsley gathered her things and headed for the exit door.

"Damn, Ainsley. Where's the fire?" Gage followed close behind. "And you don't need to take your stuff with you, we'll be back…"

She spun on him. "When we got waylaid, all you did was complain about being held up. Now you want to slow down?" Seeing the surprised expression on his face, she rolled her eyes, turned away and descended the stairs to the tarmac.

While Max again remained with the plane, a chauffeured car took them on the short ride from the airport to Harcroft headquarters in nearby San Leandro. There, she got out of the car, again carrying her tote with her.

Harcroft's headquarters was a modern structure, a marvel of steel and glass that stood out among all the other cinder-block buildings in the tech district. Entering through the front doors, whose handles were steel bass clefs, they were greeted by a friendly receptionist who was seated behind the tall, silver welcome desk. On either side of the desk, wide corridors led deeper into the building. The walls, painted a soft yellow, were accentuated by a continuous black print of horizontal lines and musical notes that made the walls look like sheet music.

Marshall Harcroft came out to greet them as they stood by the desk. Right away, Ainsley noticed the striking blue of his eyes. Wearing dark slacks, a red button-down and black loafers, he had brown hair grazing the back of his neck tucked beneath a fedora.

He stuck out his hand as he walked toward them. "Glad you folks finally made it."

Gage eyed him. "Just show us the merchandise, Marshall, and we'll be out of your hair."

"Come this way." He started walking down one of the corridors. "I think you'll be very impressed with the finished product."

They followed him down the corridor and into a room on the left side. The brightly lit room held a seating area with a small, round table and four chairs sitting around it.

Marshall remarked, "Hang tight here at the table with me for a minute, and the guys will bring your equipment for you to inspect."

The three of them took seats around the table, and she made sure they ended up with Marshall sitting between them. A few minutes passed before two men rolled in a dolly with the equipment on it. After parking the dolly next to the table, the two men accepted thanks from Marshall before disappearing the way they'd come. Gage stood, circling the soundboard as he took a closer look at it. "I see you were able to incorporate a crossfader near the center like I asked."

Marshall nodded. "What can I say? Our engineers love a challenge, and you always give them one."

Ainsley watched as the two men paced around the equipment, talking about its various features. Even though she'd worked at the recording studio for five years, she couldn't say she'd developed much of an interest in the inner workings and finer points of studio equipment. She simply took notes, as she was expected to do, by using her stylus to enter what was said into the document open on her tablet. When Gage's back was turned to her, she found herself admiring the hard lines of his buttocks and thighs beneath his slacks, and she silently cursed. *I know he's no good for me. He can't seem to tolerate children, and I have a son. I would never dream of putting a man before Cooper. If I keep staring like this, it will only make it harder to get over him.* The ringing of her phone brought her back to reality. Checking the display and seeing Bebe's name, she stood. "I have to take this. I'll go out in the hallway so I won't disturb you."

Gage nodded, barely acknowledging her exit as he and Marshall talked shop.

In the hallway, she swiped her screen. "Hey, Bebe. What's going on?"

"Not much. Cooper says he has a stomachache, so he stayed home with me today."

She frowned. "Oh no. Has he had dairy? Is there a bug going around the school?"

"Look at you, already in troubleshooting mode. He did have ice cream last night. Two bowls, if memory serves."

Ainsley rolled her eyes. "I don't know how many times he has to be laid up with the tummy ache from Hades before he realizes that his lactose intolerance is a real thing." As much as she loved Cooper, she could do without the stubborn streak he seemed to have acquired over the last few years. "Take his key, go in the medicine cabinet in the downstairs bathroom and you'll see a bottle of the pink stuff he usually takes for this."

"Roger that. I'll pop over and get it for him after we get off the phone." Bebe paused. "So, listen. I don't want to pry, but what's going on with you? I know the weather screwed up your trip plans, but what's happening now?"

She gave her neighbor a brief recap of the last thirty-six hours, leaving out that she'd slept with her boss. *No need to give up the whole operation.* "So, we finally made it here, and my boss is inspecting the equipment right now."

"Well, you don't have to rush home. Cooper's no trouble at all. Though, if I'm being honest—" she dropped her voice into a whisper, as if she didn't want to be overheard "—I think your son misses you."

A smile tipped Ainsley's lips. "Aw. I miss my little monster, too."

"I'm really impressed with this soundboard, Marshall." Gage circled the equipment one last time, stopping at the front. "Can you break down the changes and updates you've made to it?"

"We've gone digital since 404 purchased their last soundboard system from us in the early 2000s." Marshall pointed at the large device, which would easily take up a third of the floor space in the sound booth of Studio 1. "This is our top-of-the-line, custom Harcroft Diamond Edition Digital Audio Workstation."

Gage tilted his head. "It's got a big, fancy name. I hope it has capabilities to match." He really wanted to wow The Visionary and his production team when they came in to start recording.

Marshall's grin only broadened in response to the challenge in his voice. "Oh, this thing is a music-making powerhouse. You've got three monitors, our proprietary software installed to give you nearly endless sound generation possibilities, cloud-based file storage so you never run out of space to store tracks, sound effects, whatever you need. Along with that, you've got video capability, integrated editing and playback functions, and smart encryption to make it impenetrable to hackers."

"The producers will like that. Nothing spoils the buildup to an album release like leaked tracks." He scratched his chin. "Sounds like she does a lot."

"This baby will do everything except your taxes." Marshall chuckled. "That's the one feature my tech guys just couldn't figure out."

Gage laughed. "No worries. My brother Miles and his team handle all that financial stuff." A text message came through, the vibration of his phone grabbing his attention.

The message, from Nia, simply read, We have a problem. Call me.

Damn. His sister loved to pull this stunt, telling people just enough information to worry them so they'd do what she wanted. Having no idea of the nature of this problem, of course he was going to call. "Give me a sec, Marshall. Something I gotta handle right quick."

"Take your time." Marshall returned to his seat at the table as he left the room.

He passed Ainsley in the hallway, and she seemed to be on her way back to the room they'd just left. Seeing her tight expression, he asked, "Everything okay?"

She gave him a curt nod before passing by him without a word.

Shaking his head, he went to the lobby and sat down to call his older sister. When she answered, he blurted, "What is it now, Nia?"

She scoffed. "Nice greeting, little brother."

"You're the one who insisted there was a problem. So, what is it?"

She blew out a breath. "You won't believe the shit that's happened here today while you're off gallivanting."

"Sis, you are tripping. I'm not gallivanting. I'm personally escorting our business-essential equipment to its destination." He rolled his eyes, knowing she couldn't see him. "Look, why don't you just tell me what's up?"

"The Hamilton twins, that's what's up. They were here today with their mother's checkbook and an offer to buy 404 Sound."

"Pierce and London were both at our building?"

Gage blinked several times, both shocked and incensed at what he'd heard. "You can't be serious."

"I wish I weren't. They really did come in here with Everly Hamilton's checkbook, asking to meet with Mom and Dad to discuss a purchase price."

Holy crap. "I leave town for a few days and this is what goes down in my absence?" He rubbed his palm over his face. "Well, what did Mom and Dad do? I know they didn't take the meeting."

"Hell, no! Mom had security escort them off the premises." Nia laughed, the tone bitter. "But if I know the Hamiltons, this isn't over. They're not going to give up."

"You're probably right. Pierce already tried this with Dad several months back." He raked his hand through his hair. "Shit. I need to get back there."

"You're damn straight, and sooner is better. Dad is sullen and Mom is pissed. Odds are we're going to be called to some kind of meeting to discuss next steps in shaking off Hamilton House and their takeover attempts."

That's exactly what this is, a takeover attempt. He didn't know if their tactics qualified as hostile, but they sure as hell seemed determined to take ownership of the Woodson family's legacy. "Okay. I need to wrap things up here by signing off on the equipment and getting it back to the private jet. Hopefully, I'll be back in Atlanta before nine." He knew they'd lose three hours in the air traveling from west to east.

"Fine. Just text me when you land. See you later, Gage."

"Bye, sis." After he disconnected the call, he stood and walked back down the corridor, returning to the room with Marshall, Ainsley and his shiny new soundboard.

"I've briefed your assistant on all the details." Marshall clapped his hands together. "So, I'm ready to move forward with paperwork whenever you are."

Gage looked at Ainsley, seated at the table with her tablet in front of her and the stylus in hand.

Without looking up from her screen, she said, "I've taken detailed notes on all the pertinent information, sir."

He frowned. *Sir? When did we get back on such formal terms?* After the passion they'd shared, he would never have imagined she'd be back to referring to him that way. But he didn't want to cause a scene by asking her about it now. They were working, and there was no reason Marshall should be privy to their private affairs. So instead, he simply nodded. "Thank you."

"Well, I'm going to pop over to my office for the tablet so you can digitally sign the forms and take delivery." Marshall walked toward the door. "Feel free to play with the controls until I get back. Just don't do anything crazy or you'll void the warranty." With a grin, he disappeared through the door.

Alone with Ainsley, Gage could no longer hold

back his curiosity. "Ainsley, why are you back to calling me *sir*?"

She shrugged. "We're working, aren't we? I'm just focused on the job right now."

"Oh, that's nice. But it doesn't explain why you were so snappy toward me on the plane." He watched her expectantly, awaiting her answer.

She groaned. "I'm not going to talk about this with you right now, Gage."

He walked closer to her, placing a gentle hand on her forearm. "But, baby…"

She drew away from him. "Don't call me that, Gage." Her eyes flashed, but behind the anger, he could see hints of pain.

"What's going on with you? Is it something I did? Or something I said? Because…"

"Save it." She shook her head. "I can't believe you don't know what the problem is."

He cringed. Apparently, she found him not only annoying but dense at this juncture. "Just tell me what I did so I can at least try to fix it."

She turned her back to him. "As I said, we're not talking about this right now."

He stood there watching her, not knowing what else to say. Their night together had been special… at least to him. Had it all been some kind of game to her? He'd taken a chance and now she was making a fool of him.

Just like Tara had.

Thirteen

"So, does the equipment meet your standards?" Marshall returned to the room, a large tablet tucked under his arm.

Gage took a huge step back, turning his attention away from Ainsley to respond to the question. "Yeah, everything looks great. We just need to get it loaded onto a truck and taken to the airport so we can get it on the jet and back to Atlanta."

"It's already arranged." Marshall turned on the tablet, the screen illuminating as he pulled a stylus from his pocket. "As soon as we're done with the forms, I'll just put in a quick call for my staff to bring the truck around, and you can ride to the airport with them if you like."

"Thanks." Gage scratched his chin. "You know if you had sold the equipment from under me, this would have been a totally different kind of meeting."

Marshall chuckled. "Well, I did promise you I'd hold it for three days, and I'm a man of my word."

From observing their interactions after years of overhearing their phone calls, Ainsley could see that Marshall and Gage had a strange sort of kinship. As two men in adjacent fields, they didn't need to compete with each other. But that didn't stop them from ribbing each other whenever they had the chance.

She watched in silence as Marshall walked Gage through the electronic forms, having him sign and initial in all the proper places. With that done, the truck was summoned.

The truck pulled around to the front of the building about a half hour after Gage had begun filling out the forms. A crew of three men helped to wrap and secure the equipment for shipment and, using a ramp, loaded it onto the back of the box truck and shut the door. Ainsley watched all this from a safe distance, wondering how to say what she had to say to Gage.

"I'm going to text Max and let her know we're on our way back to the plane." As the men loaded the equipment, Gage headed for the cab, typing on his phone as he walked. "Ainsley, you don't mind catching a ride with the truck driver, do you?"

She took a deep breath. "No." She had so many things she wanted to get off her chest. But standing in the parking lot of their equipment supplier, she knew better than to get into all that with him. It wasn't the time or the place.

They got into the cab of the truck, with her sitting in the middle, just as she had in Hugh Delmar's truck, and rode to the airport. She was thankful that the drive was less than ten minutes, because she didn't want the awkward silence hanging between her and Gage to stretch on for any longer than necessary. *That's why I can't get back on the company jet with him.*

As the truck rolled onto the tarmac, she could see Max, waving to them from her spot near the plane. The pilot's all-black uniform and red-and-black bow tie were immaculate as always, and her braids were pulled back into a neat bun. Ainsley sighed. *As much as I like Max, I'm not excited about this trip.*

Ainsley did her part to make sure the equipment was safely loaded and properly secured on the plane, clutching her tote bag the entire time. Once the job was done, Gage started walking up the steps to board the jet. He glanced back at her, still standing on the ground. "Come on, Ainsley, get the lead out. We need to get back."

She swallowed. *I wish I could afford to fly commercial. The last thing I want right now is to be trapped with him for four hours.* Alas, her wallet wept at the thought of paying the price of a last-minute plane ticket, so she finally got her feet moving and climbed the stairs.

Once they were back in the air, she found herself

staring out the window, at the ceiling, the floor—anything to avoid looking at Gage.

From his seat across the aisle, he said, "I spoke to Nia earlier. She said the Hamilton twins came by today and tried to buy the company."

Even though her interest was minimal, she knew any sale of the business could possibly affect her current job or her ability to make the move into human resources. So, she engaged, despite the fact she didn't want to talk to him. "Oh, really?"

She half listened while he talked about the Hamilton family's attempts to take ownership of 404 Sound. Mostly, she found herself staring at his lips, the same full lips that had kissed her in her most intimate places just last night.

"From listening to Nia, I can't tell if she's more upset about the whole takeover thing, or the fact they just skipped over her to ask for Mom and Dad. Nia is the CEO, and it's not like a deal could go down without her."

"Yeah." She watched him gesture with his hands, the hands that had gripped her hips as he took her to paradise. She cursed her hormones for trying to override her good sense and went back to looking out the window.

"I…uh…feel like I'm losing you, Ainsley."

"No," she insisted, still staring into the endless blue void. "I'm still listening."

"That's not what I meant."

The tone of his voice made her turn back to look

at his face again. The moment their eyes met, she regretted her decision but found she couldn't look away.

"I feel like I've really put myself on the line here, Ainsley." He rubbed his hands together as he spoke. "I've broken my own personal pledge not to get romantically involved with a colleague. And for a while there, I thought it had all been worth it."

She swallowed, feeling the irritation rise within her. *There he goes again, martyring himself, talking about what he's been inconvenienced with. He's so selfish sometimes. He never thinks of the consequences of his words.* "You aren't the only one taking a risk here, Gage."

"It certainly feels that way. I mean, you haven't even expressed your feelings to me." He paused, a small but wicked grin tilting the corner of his mouth. "Well, at least not with words."

She could feel her lips tightening. *He thinks awfully highly of himself, though that's nothing new.*

"Either way, I'd rather have you tell me than to assume." He cracked his knuckles, one by one, as he continued. "Just be honest with me, Ainsley. Tell me what's on your mind."

She narrowed her eyes, feeling the southwest Atlanta fire rising within her. "Oh, trust me. You're about to get every bit of this smoke."

Gage felt his shoulders tense up in response to Ainsley's terse words. "What?"

"You wanna know how I feel, right? Then you better guard your grill, because it ain't nothing nice." She folded her arms over her chest and glared at him.

He was used to Ainsley speaking to him in such professional tones that hearing her talk this way took him by surprise. "Are you serious right now, Ainsley? After the ordeal we went through just trying to get here, you're going to hit me with this. Now? When we're finally almost home?"

"The timing may not be the best, but it is what it is, Gage."

"Okay, I don't like the sound of that, but I do want to know what's going on. What is your problem? You've been acting strangely all day."

"What you see as me acting strangely is simply self-preservation."

Gage pressed his fingertips to his temple. "I don't mean to sound dismissive, but that makes literally no sense at all."

"Really, Gage?" She rolled her eyes. "You spent the entire time in Summer Village looking down on the people there."

He frowned. "No, I didn't. I barely interacted with them."

"I know. And that was by design. At the times when you did interact with them, I saw your attitude. You were so annoyed that this charming little town didn't have your soy lattes and Wi-Fi."

He sighed. "I'll admit that. I'm a city boy to the core, and I—"

"Nah. It's more than that. I grew up in the city, too, but only one of us grew up spoiled, having their every whim catered to."

That remark hit him right in the chest, and if the smug look on her face were any indication, that had been her intention. "That's not fair, Ainsley. My parents worked extremely hard to build 404 and give us a decent life."

"Which is why you should have a better attitude." With her upper body turned toward him, she leaned in, her glare slicing through him even from across the aisle. "But you know what's worse than your attitude?"

"No, but I'm sure you're gonna tell me." He let his head drop back against his seat.

"Your absolute intolerance of children. Why do you dislike them so much?"

"I never said that."

"You didn't have to. It was written all over your face every time you spoke about children." She shook her head. "Remember, I was there last week when those schoolkids came to visit the office. You were cordial at first, but the minute one of them said something you didn't like, your whole demeanor changed. It seemed like you couldn't get out of there fast enough."

That was true, but not for the reasons she thought. "Listen, I'll admit I'm not comfortable around kids. But I don't—"

She cut him off. "And then this morning, while

we're supposed to be enjoying the afterglow of love-making, you start to get chatty. And since I want to know about your childhood, and you've never opened up to me like this, I let you talk. And what do you do? You go on and on about the misery you must have caused your parents, simply by existing."

He swallowed, his throat dry. "I didn't mean it like that. I just…"

"I know you're about to give me some lame excuse, but don't bother. I'm a single mother, Gage. And while my son exhausts both my energy and my finances, he's been an absolute joy to raise."

He held up his hand. "Wait, Ainsley. You can't think I was talking about Cooper. I wasn't. I was only speaking in general."

"It doesn't matter. It's not about the words so much as the attitude behind them." She shook her head, feeling the tears spring to her eyes. "To think I let myself get wrapped up with you like this. I can't believe I let you get so close, knowing how you felt about children." The tears welled in her eyes. "I can't do this, Gage. I can't risk my heart for someone who wouldn't accept my son."

He closed his eyes, his sadness morphing into frustration. "You know what, Ainsley? You're being unreasonable."

Her eyes flashed, and she pointed to herself. "Oh, *I'm* unreasonable, huh? Me. I'm the one that's out of step here."

He could hear his tone changing to match the

darkness of his mood, but he no longer cared. "Absolutely. You're entirely too sensitive. You take everything I say in passing and twist it around to fit your little agenda, to make me out to be the bad guy."

"Oh, and why is that? Since you suddenly know everything about the way I think and operate." She tilted her head until it almost touched her shoulder, staring at him, her lips pursed.

He shook his head, chuckling bitterly. "You're not trying to hear it."

"Nah, don't stop now. You're on a roll." She clapped her hands together. "Enlighten me, Gage. Why am I acting so sensitive? Tell me more about my li'l agenda."

If the situation weren't so tense, he'd be amused at the lengths she took to goad him into answering. "You really wanna know?"

"Hell, yeah, Gage. I *really* wanna know."

He inhaled. "You're scared. You can't commit, and you're using your kid as an easy excuse to avoid letting me into your life." He paused. "You've probably been doing it for years. I can't be the first one who's tried to love you." The minute he'd finished, he realized how harsh his words must have sounded. "Look, I didn't…"

"Don't." She closed her eyes for several long moments. When she opened them again, the fire was gone, replaced with a coldness that nearly made him shiver. "You know what, Gage? I'm gonna put on my headphones now. And it would be wise if you didn't say another single word to me for the rest of this flight."

"Baby, listen. I just…"

She held up her finger. "Don't you dare 'baby' me. Whatever happened between us in Summer Village can stay there. It's strictly business from now on. Now please, just leave me alone." She popped in her earbuds, plugged them into her phone and rested her head against her seat, her gazed focused out the window.

He sighed. He'd thought they were finally getting somewhere, that he could finally share his affection with someone. But it seemed fate enjoyed making a fool of him, again and again. Not even the luxurious surroundings of the private jet could remove the awkwardness and tension hanging in the air. But he knew better than to try to engage her again, so he simply closed his eyes and tried to sleep for the remainder of the flight.

I thought we had something special. Now it's over before it even began.

Fourteen

Friday afternoon, Ainsley sat on the bleachers at Carter G. Woodson's baseball field, watching the game. Her son and the rest of the Roaring Lions were up against the Fulton Leadership Bears, their old rival. The orange-and-blue uniforms worn by the home team were already streaked with soil and grass stains, as were the red-and-white uniforms of the opposition. The young men played hard. It was as if they were all bucking for a place in the major leagues. As they headed into the seventh inning, Ainsley stifled a yawn.

Bebe, sitting next to her, gave her a soft poke in the shoulder. "Wake up, Ainsley. Game's not over yet."

Ainsley gave her a little half smile. "I'll try. But to tell you the truth, I'm exhausted."

"I noticed. Ever since you came back from your work trip, you've seemed a little down." Bebe gave her shoulder a squeeze. "I'm not one to pry, as you know. But if you decide you want someone to talk to, I'm here. I know it's probably been hard on you since your cousin moved out."

"Thanks, Bebe." Ainsley inhaled deeply, taking in the scents of grass, dirt and two dozen sweaty preteens. Bebe was right on both counts. She had been down since she got back from California, and she missed Eden terribly. Still, she wouldn't begrudge her cousin the happiness she'd found when she married Gage's brother Blaine.

She hadn't had a decent night's sleep since her return, and having to go to work and see Gage every day, knowing what they'd shared and what they could never have, was exhausting mentally and emotionally. The lack of sleep, coupled with her usual activity level, had drained her physically. Basically, she was tired in all the ways a person could be tired. Putting on her best fake smile in case Cooper looked at her, she directed her attention back to the game.

The Lions were ahead, and she joined the other families in cheering them on. She fought off the urge to wave at Cooper or make any kind of spectacle of herself, knowing he was in the thick of the "everything my mom does is embarrassing" phase. Aside from that, she knew she probably looked a hot mess.

She'd thrown on an old pair of medium-wash jeans and a Carter G. Woodson Academy PTA sweatshirt. Her hair was in a haphazard knot low on her neck, and she'd crammed her feet into a pair of old sneakers as she rushed out the door, bent on getting Cooper to the field in time. Their coach demanded that they arrive thirty minutes prior to all games or spend the game guarding the dugout. Today, she'd just barely gotten him there on time.

"Look at Bryce! That's the second run he's scored tonight!" Bebe stood, clapping furiously for her son.

Ainsley shook her head. While she was proud of Cooper's athletic accomplishments, his academic ones held much more weight in her mind. Still, her son didn't want her cheering for him at debate meets, either. So, she'd learned to hold on to the praise she wanted to heap on him until they were alone at home. That way she could hug him, and maybe even give him a peck on the cheek, without him making too much of a fuss about it.

In the end, the Lions trounced the Bears, and the parents joined Coach Rigsby and the team on the field for a congratulatory pep talk. When the coach released them, Bebe announced that they were headed out for a celebratory pizza party. Ainsley smiled and cheered along with everyone else, though inside, she wanted nothing more than to go home, burrow under her covers and sleep until Monday.

At the pizza place, Ainsley sat at one end of the table with Bebe and another team mom. The three of them were tasked with chaperoning the fourteen adolescents as they gorged on pizza and soda and, later, making sure all of them made it home safely. She ate her own slice of pepperoni slowly, thinking as she chewed. While her eyes rested on the boys, who were currently huddled around one teammate's phone watching goofy videos on the internet, her mind was elsewhere. She kept replaying the argument she'd had with Gage. She remembered how angry she'd been, and how that anger had melted into total awkwardness as she spent the rest of the flight trying to pretend he didn't even exist. Being trapped with him on the plane had made the whole conversation all the more difficult to have.

In a way, she was glad it had happened, or so she told herself. By giving him a huge piece of her mind, she'd saved herself further heartache down the line. She couldn't imagine how much worse it would have been for her if she waited, fell deeper in love and really let him in, only to have him disappoint her.

Her heart clenched. She missed his touch, and it was driving her nuts. It made no sense. They'd shared several steamy hours in bed in a tiny town down South, and now she just couldn't go back to the way things were. She'd still see him at work every day, and she didn't see that changing unless she got the HR manager job. That's what had prompted her to apply first thing Thursday morning. No more excuses. She needed this change.

Feeling the tears welling up in her eyes, she excused herself and went to the restroom. *If Bebe sees me crying, she'll start asking questions, and she won't stop badgering me until she gets to the bottom of it.*

In the privacy of a stall, she leaned against the wall and let the tears flow. Keeping her sobs quiet in case someone walked in, she pressed a ball of tissue to her face. *I'm so pitiful. Here I am, locked in a bathroom stall, crying like a high schooler.*

Blowing out a breath, she left the stall.

And almost ran into Bebe.

She closed her eyes. "Bebe, please. Don't ask."

Bebe nodded. "All right." She stepped aside and let Ainsley pass.

At the sink, she washed her face and hands, then held a cool, damp paper towel to her eyes in an attempt to reduce the puffiness. Then, with Bebe still watching her warily, she exited the restroom and returned to the table.

Later, as she leaned over Cooper's bed to kiss him good-night, he called her. "Mom?"

"What is it, sweetie?"

"Are you okay?" He watched her, concern filling his dark eyes.

"What makes you ask that?"

He shrugged. "I don't know. You just seem… sad." He paused, his expression turning serious. "Did somebody do something to you? Do I need to beat somebody up?"

She felt the smile stretch her lips. *My baby.* "No,

Cooper. While I love that you want to protect me, I don't need you to beat anyone up. I'm just working through some complex adult feelings, but I'll be fine once I get it figured out."

His tone earnest, he asked, "Promise?"

She nodded. "I promise." She leaned down and gave him a second peck on the cheek. "Good night, Coop."

"'Night, Mom." He snuggled down under the covers.

Turning out the light, she left his room, closing the door behind her. As she sought her own bed, she couldn't help thinking that everyone around her seemed to be able to tell she was upset.

Get it together, girl. She'd gotten to enjoy the fantasy of Gage as her boyfriend for a little while. Now it was time to abandon that fallacy and go back to thinking of him as her boss.

Stifling a yawn, she crawled into bed.

Gage sat at the table in 404's main conference room Friday evening, drumming his fingers on the table. It was already after six, and it was rare for the executive team to even be at work this late, let alone sitting in an emergency meeting.

Around the table, the entire Woodson family was assembled. Nia sat at the head, with their parents flanking her. Miles and Teagan were sitting on Dad's side, while Blaine and Gage were on Mom's side.

The other end of the table was occupied by the enigmatic, rarely-seen-in-public Everly Hamilton.

What Gage knew about the older woman could fit into a bottle cap. He knew that his parents had known Everly for years and had even considered her and her late husband good friends. He also knew that she'd become something of a recluse over the last decade, preferring to send her children or her assistants out in public to do her bidding.

Gage couldn't help staring at her, but at least he tried to keep his attention discreet. She wore a black dress beneath a huge white fur coat. Her short-cropped hair, dyed platinum blond, was swept dramatically across her forehead and teased at the crown. She was somewhat fair in complexion, but very obviously African American. Huge designer sunglasses obscured much of her face, until she reached up, her red manicured nails grasping the arm. She pulled them off, revealing two penetrating gray eyes. "Woodson family. How nice of you to take time out of your busy schedules to meet with me."

Gage was taken aback by the depth of her voice; it didn't seem to match her appearance. He could only attribute the tone to years of smoking.

Addison scoffed. "You're a real piece of work, Everly."

"I'll take that as a compliment coming from you, *old* friend." She leaned forward as she placed emphasis on the word *old*.

Addison's eyes flashed.

Caleb grabbed his wife's hand. "Look, we didn't come here for any immature foolishness. We're tired of you sending your little lackeys here to do your dirty work."

"You mean the twins? How dare you refer to my babies that way." Everly slapped the table.

"Oh please. They're both adults," Nia interjected. "Though I'm not sure they know much about anything, beyond parroting your words."

Everly laughed, a sort of croaking sound. "Whatever. I think it's high time you kids had a little history lesson." She locked eyes with Caleb. "Don't you think so, Caleb?"

Gage watched his father's jaw tighten.

"Don't act as if my opinion matters," Caleb groused. "You're just going to do what you want anyway."

"How astute of you." Everly cleared her throat, settling back in her chair. "Let's take a little trip down memory lane. Years back, before any of you were born, your father and my boyfriend Philip were the best of friends. Their friendship created one between Addy and me, since we were dating the boys at the time, and we were together pretty much all the time."

Teagan tilted her head. "Phil. I've heard that name before."

Everly continued. "Over the years, our bond deepened, and Addy and I were privy to the boys' dream. They talked about wanting to build the best, most state-of-the-art recording studio in Atlanta. The city was experiencing a creative boom, and it seemed new hip-hop and R & B artists were coming out of every neighborhood. Phil and Caleb worked on their plan together for several years, through our college career and the beginning of our marriages."

Gage scratched his chin. He followed the story, but what he didn't understand was what any of this had to do with Everly's attempts to take over the business. His mind wandered then, back to the same subject it had been wandering to since he'd gotten back from California.

Ainsley. He missed her. The past two days in the office hadn't been the same. Things had definitely changed between them, and he knew they couldn't go back to the working relationship they had before. He was fine with that, but what bothered him was the idea that he'd never get to see what it was like to be her man. They'd danced around their attraction for so long, and when they'd finally connected romantically, he'd managed to screw it up. He wanted to kick himself. Shaking off the thoughts as best he could, he tried to refocus on Everly's story.

"Then, I got pregnant." Everly's tone darkened. "It threw a wrench in the plan. We needed money, and Phil vowed to do right by me and take care of our babies. And so he set his dream aside, placing it in Caleb's hands while he joined up with the marines." She paused, touching her hand to her chest.

"He only served eight months before he was killed in a training exercise at Camp Mayfield."

Miles shifted in his seat. "I'm sorry for your loss, Mrs. Hamilton."

Everyone around the table added their condolences, though Caleb was oddly silent.

"Thank you, all of you. But that's not where the story ends." Everly brushed away a tear. "Did your father ever tell you where half his start-up capital came from? The money he used to purchase the first studio?"

Nia shook her head. "No, and to be honest, I never thought to ask."

Everly inhaled deeply. "Philip. He willed that a portion of his death benefit be paid to Caleb if anything should happen to him."

All eyes in the room turned toward Caleb, who looked as if he wanted a trapdoor to open in the floor and consume him.

Tears welled in Addison's eyes. "How could you keep that from me, Caleb?"

Everly's perfectly sculpted brow rose. "You didn't know?"

Addison shook her head. "I had no idea. But that explains why you've been so interested in the company."

"Maybe now you understand where I'm coming from." Everly raked a hand through her hair. "I lost my husband, but I had two things to keep his spirit with me—our babies and his dream. I'll admit I've taken too strong an approach, but all I really want is to be a part of the thing he was so passionate about."

Caleb sighed. "I'm sorry, Addy. I should have told you. But at the time, I just wanted to be the hero. I needed you to think I'd done this on my own."

Gage blinked. *This is wild.* He would never have expected his father to pull something like this. Glancing at his siblings' faces around the table, he could see that they all looked similarly shocked.

Caleb continued. "And Everly, I'm sorry I dishonored Philip's legacy by not including you and the twins." He looked genuinely contrite. "I'm still not going to sell you the company. But I'm willing to sell you a stake."

"Majority?" Everly tilted her head.

"Don't push it, Ev." Caleb shook his head. "How does thirty percent sound?"

Everly appeared to think it over for a few moments.

Everyone waited in silence for her response.

Finally, she countered, "Thirty-five."

"Thirty-two." That came from Addison, who eyed Everly intently.

"Deal."

Both women rose from their seats and met near the center of the table, sealing the deal with a handshake.

"One more thing, Everly." Addison still clutched her hand. "We'd really like it if you, Pierce and London would take part in the anniversary celebration we're having later this year."

Everly appeared genuinely touched. "Do you mean it, Addy?"

Addison nodded. "Absolutely. It's only right."

"Then we'll be there." Everly gave her hand a squeeze.

Gage blew out a breath, relieved that this meeting had gone in a positive direction. Seeing the way things had unfolded made him think.

If these three can heal from a decades-old mistake, maybe there's still hope for Ainsley and me.

Fifteen

Ainsley trudged to the kitchen table Saturday morning, clutching her favorite mug filled with coffee. Clad in an old pair of leggings, an oversize T-shirt and bunny slippers, she rubbed her eyes with her free hand as she walked. Pulling out her chair, she sat down and took in the scene.

Cooper, wearing an old T-shirt and basketball shorts, walked over with a bowl of cereal and a glass of orange juice. "Here you go, Mom."

She smiled. "Thank you, baby." To her mind, this was better than a fancy breakfast at a five-star restaurant. Her son had made it for her, and she knew he'd done so with love.

"I made toast, too. Let me go get it." He dashed

off, returning with a piece of wheat toast on a small saucer. "I buttered it for you." He sat down across from her with his own food.

"I really appreciate this." She marveled at her child's thoughtfulness as she ate. Though he had his moments where her affection embarrassed him, deep down, he still wanted to take care of his mother. *I must've done something right with his raising.*

When they'd finished, he cleared away the dishes. "Ready to get started?"

"Sure." She got up and went to fix herself a second cup of coffee.

Cooper moved back and forth across the room until he'd placed everything he needed on the table. The supplies for his school project were spread across the tabletop. There was water, flour, salt, paint, brushes and a large foam-core poster board.

"Do you have the paper with the instructions on it?" She stifled a yawn.

"Right here, Mom." He held up a white sheet with typed instructions on it. He began reading aloud. "'Students are to create a full-color salt dough map of a fictional country that includes the following landforms: river, lake, ocean, mountain, valley, plateau, island and beach.'"

"That's a lot of landforms." She took a long swig from her coffee cup. "Have you drawn a diagram yet?"

He shook his head. "No. Do I need one?"

"I think you do." She stretched. "Salt dough dries

fast. So, by the time you start, you already need to know everything you're doing and how it's going to be laid out." She gestured to his notebook, lying on the counter. "Go get some paper, draw out the whole surface of your country and mark where all your landforms are going to be. That's gonna help out a lot when you get ready to sculpt."

He got up to get his notebook, and she drained a considerable portion of her coffee. *Come on, caffeine. Don't fail me now.* She'd slept slightly better last night than the previous two nights, but that wasn't saying much. And having to get up early this morning to fulfill her promise to help Cooper with his project meant she couldn't linger in bed.

An image of Gage came into her mind, and she pushed it away. She'd spent enough time thinking about him. Now she needed to focus on Cooper and his project. Her son deserved her full attention, and she planned to give it to him.

She stood behind Cooper's chair, providing guidance as he used a pencil to sketch out his fictional country. "It looks really good so far, Cooper. What are you going to call your country?"

"Hmm. I don't know yet." He kept sketching, adding in the small details to the larger shape he'd drawn. "I probably won't know till I'm finished and I get a good look at it, ya know?"

"Fair enough." She finished her coffee and went to put the mug in the sink.

"You know what Bryce is calling his country?"

"No, what?"

"New Redford."

She chuckled, wondering if Bebe had helped her son name his country. While she washed up the breakfast dishes, he worked quietly at the table, finishing up the diagram of his fictional land. He held it up for her to see as she returned to the table. "What do you think, Mom?"

"Looks good. Let me see that paper." She took his instruction sheet, comparing the list of required landforms to the ones depicted on his drawing. "Awesome. You've included all eight landforms. I think we're good to go on mixing the dough."

"Cool." He slid the bowls of flour and salt closer to him. "Do we need to measure this out?"

"We could, but I did this same project as a kid." She picked up the pitcher of water. "I think we're good to just eyeball it. First, dump that little bowl of salt in with the flour." Cooper did as she asked, and she handed him a rubber spatula. "Okay. Now you stir while I add the water."

She added water slowly, watching him mix, until the consistency of the mix looked about right to her. Setting the pitcher aside, she said, "Now, here's the messy part. Get in there with your hands and work it into a dough ball."

She watched Cooper do just that until he was left with a pretty sizable lump of dough. "How's this?"

"Great. Now we'll start sculpting." Using the poster board as a base, they spread out the dough, forming and shaping it to be as close a match as possible to the diagram he'd drawn.

He placed the small island off the coast and flattened it out, stepping back from their creation. "How long will it take to dry?"

A knock at the door interrupted her before she could answer. "I'll be right back." Going to the front door, she checked the peephole. Smiling, she opened the door. "Eden! It's good to see you, cousin."

Eden, dressed in dark skinny jeans and a sunny yellow tunic, stepped inside, immediately engulfing Ainsley in a hug. "I missed y'all, so I decided to come hang for a while."

"Come on in the kitchen. We're working on a school project."

In the kitchen, Ainsley watched as Cooper ran to hug his favorite cousin. "What do you think of my project?"

Eden eyed the board, confused. "It's great. Now… what is it supposed to be?"

Cooper laughed. "It's a country. It'll look better after I paint it."

"Sounds good." She squeezed his shoulder. "Listen. Why don't you take a break while this dries so your mom and I can chat?"

Ainsley interjected, "Yeah. I think that's a good idea. Go on next door and see what Bryce is up to, but be back in an hour."

After Cooper left, the two of them sat on the couch, drinking iced tea. Eden set her glass down and faced Ainsley. "Okay. I can tell something's bothering you, so spill it."

Taking a deep breath, Ainsley recounted what had transpired between her and Gage, including their argument on the flight back from California. "And just like that, it was over. I barely got to enjoy the high of being with him before reality hit, hard."

Eden sighed. "Oh, honey. I feel your pain here, and I hate to see you hurt. Do you want my advice, or did you just want me to listen?"

"If you have advice, I'll take it." She welcomed a solution to her Gage problem since she couldn't seem to come up with one on her own.

"Let him be the bigger person. You're right to be cautious about whom you bring around your son, and if he can't see that, then he's not the man for you."

"That sounds so sensible."

"Because it is."

Ainsley chuckled. "Remember all those months back, when you pointed out my crush on him and told me to do something about it?"

Eden nodded. "I remember. But trust me, this isn't how I anticipated it turning out."

With a deep sigh, Ainsley admitted, "Looks like time has made fools of us all."

"Well, that was dramatic." Eden grabbed her hand, squeezing it. "Either he'll come to his senses and apologize, or he won't, and you'll know it's not meant to be."

She let her head drop onto Eden's shoulder. "Thanks for the advice, E."

"Anytime, honey."

Saturday afternoon, Gage jogged the trail at Piedmont Park, doing his best to keep up with his brother Blaine. Despite the way he'd been feeling the past few days, he was determined to keep up his fitness routine. The first half of the week was still wearing on him, affecting his sleep and his ability to concentrate. Now more than ever, he needed the endorphins to boost his mood.

Blaine, a longtime runner, seemed to be taking great pleasure in leaving him behind. His long strides carried him over the bumpy terrain of the trail with ease, like a gazelle crossing the savannah.

Gage panted, knowing he probably looked more like a giraffe loping through the forest. "I said we were jogging, Blaine," he called out. "Not running."

"Can't keep up, bro?" he called over his shoulder.

"Isn't that obvious? Now slow down!" Gage stopped, placing his palm against a tree trunk to grab a few moments of rest.

Blaine finally slowed, then turned around and jogged back to the tree where Gage stood. "You all right?"

He shook his head. "We talked about this, dude. I'm not a runner. Listen, can we just walk the rest of the trail?"

Blaine eyed him for a moment before relenting.

"Sure, that's fine. I don't wanna have to take you to the ER."

"Angel of mercy." Gage took a few more deep breaths, then the two of them started walking the trail.

They walked a short distance in silence, and Gage finally got a moment to enjoy the scenery. A squirrel scurried across the path, leaving a trail of acorn shells in his wake. The thick canopy of trees shaded them from the sunlit sky above, the air heavy with the scent. There were magnolias, dogwoods, mimosa. Piedmont Park was home to around 115 species of trees, and a seasonally warm, blue-sky day like this was the perfect day to take in the sights.

Still, he couldn't enjoy it the way he normally would. Though surrounded by natural beauty of all kinds, he saw Ainsley's face everywhere he looked. He heard her voice on the wind, whispering his name. To say he missed her would be a gross understatement. Seeing her at work just wasn't the same. He wanted to be more than her boss, more than just a friend she knew from work.

Fat chance of that now that I've screwed up so royally. He sighed.

Blaine looked his way. "Man, what's the matter with you?"

"What makes you think something is wrong?"

"Are you kidding? You just literally deep sighed. Aside from that, last night, while we were all learning an epic secret about the beginnings of our fam-

ily's company, you looked completely spaced out."
Blaine poked him in the shoulder. "We grew up together, and you think I can't tell when you're upset?"

Gage sighed again. He and Blaine were the closest
in age, the middle sons who often played together,
went to school together and got into trouble together.
"If I tell you, you have to promise not to be judg-
mental about it."

"Whew. That bad, huh?" He pointed at a bench
up ahead. "Maybe we'd better sit down for this one,
then."

When they reached the bench and sat down,
Blaine said, "I'm listening."

"Tell me how you and Eden are doing first."

A broad grin spread across his face at the mention
of his wife's name. "We're amazing. She's amazing.
Waking up with her every morning makes my life
so much better. I mean, she has this little thing she
does when she's asleep and…"

Gage held up his hand. "Okay, a little of that goes
a long way. Much more and I'm gonna barf." Teasing was his only recourse here. He loved knowing
that his brother was so happy, but he couldn't help
feeling a twinge of jealousy as well. "So, let's pivot
to my problem now."

"All right, all right." Blaine feigned offense. "Go
ahead."

"So, it's about this trip I took with my assistant
to pick up the equipment…"

"C'mon, man. You say 'my assistant' as if Ainsley and I don't go way back." Blaine shook his head. "Man. I wonder if I could ever get her back in the studio. Not many girls who are so confident singing alto." He paused, tilted his head, and stared at him. "Wait a minute."

Gage swallowed.

Blaine's eyes grew wide. "Oh shit. Y'all didn't…"

Gage closed his eyes against his brother's accusing stare. He knew what Blaine had been about to say, so he responded in kind. "Yeah, we did."

"Oh wow." Blaine shook his head. "Man. I know you had a thing for her for a while, but…"

"Wait. How did you know about that?"

"Bro, we all know." Blaine scoffed. "I mean, all your siblings know. I don't think Mom and Dad are around the offices enough to be aware, but we all know."

"How?" He knew that his father knew. He didn't want to think his attractions were on display at such a level that everybody else could see them.

"Easy. Anybody who's spent more than ten minutes in the room with the two of you can see it. I mean, she likes you back, so…" He stopped. "So y'all finally sealed the deal. I'd think you'd both be happy. So, what happened?"

He recapped the argument they'd had. "She was high-key pissed at me, and she told me that any chance of a romantic relationship between us was dead."

Blaine scratched his chin. "Hmm. Let's just take a look at what she said. She thinks you hate children."

"Basically. I tried to tell her that's not true, but she wasn't hearing none of it."

"Well, I mean..." Blaine twisted his lips.

"What? Don't tell me you think I hate kids, too."

"Nah. I think it's more like a phobia."

Gage glared.

Blaine laughed. "Sorry, sorry. Anyway, what I mean is you just don't seem to know what to do when you're around kids, so you default to this kind of grouchy personality."

He ran a hand over his head. "So, you're saying there's some truth in what she said."

"There is. The question is, what are you gonna do about it?"

Gage inhaled deeply, thinking about it. "I don't really know. I guess my first step is to get to the root of it, because I can't really give a reason why being around kids makes me so nervous."

Blaine nodded approvingly. "Now we're getting somewhere. Self-reflection is always a good thing."

He made a mental note to start looking for a therapist when he got back home. "That's one step that will help me. I still need to figure out what I can do to get Ainsley to give me another chance, though."

Blaine released a wry chuckle. "Oh, I've got some experience with being in the wrong. My advice is to start with a sincere apology. Then let her know that you're working through your issues around children and parenthood."

"That sounds like a levelheaded approach. What happens if she still won't hear me out?"

He shrugged. "I guess you'll just have to accept that it wasn't meant to be. I don't think it'll come to that, though. From what I know of Ainsley, she'll probably give you a shot."

"I hope you're right, B. I really hope you're right."

A few minutes later, they got to their feet and continued down the trail.

Sixteen

Ainsley rolled out of bed Sunday morning around ten. It was the first time she'd slept for more than three hours, and she felt surprisingly good—physically anyway. She checked on Cooper and found him lying in bed playing a game on his e-reader. Satisfied that he was occupied for the time being, she returned to her room and took a hot shower.

Refreshed and clean, she dressed in a pair of clean black leggings and her black Pretty Girls Like Trap Music sweatshirt that she'd bought from the merch table at a 2 Chainz concert. Tying an old pink bandanna over her hair, she stepped into her bunny slippers and headed downstairs for her usual Sunday routine: cleaning and lounging. On the way down, she stopped by her son's room again and peeked inside.

Without looking up from his game, he said, "I know, Mom. Change my sheets, clean my room and clean the upstairs bathroom."

She smiled. In spite of the slight annoyance in his tone, at least he knew what his responsibilities were. "Good boy. I'll come up and check on you in a couple of hours."

She had a bagel and a cup of coffee for breakfast. A glance in the sink let her know that Cooper had already had cereal, so she didn't need to interrupt his gaming to offer him food. After she'd eaten, she pulled her cleaning caddy out from under the cabinet and set it on the counter. Setting her small wireless speaker to stream a classic soul station from her phone, she started clearing the clutter from her counters and table.

By the time she wiped down the counters, she was dancing with the broom to the tune of an old Barry White song. Something about her Sunday cleaning ritual made her feel renewed, and today was no different. She'd rid the house of the grime accumulated during the past week and, hopefully, do the same for her mind.

After mopping the kitchen floor, she grabbed her caddy and her speaker, carrying them with her into the living room. Setting everything down on the coffee table, she began by picking up the random trash scattered around the room.

She was carrying a handful of Cooper's discarded snack wrappers to the trash can when she heard a pounding sound. At first, she thought it was the bass line of the New Birth song playing on her speaker, but when she stopped and listened, she realized someone was knocking at the front door. Assuming it was Bebe coming over for a gab session, she strode over and opened the door.

Her mouth fell open when she saw Gage standing on her doorstep. His expression contrite, he held a bouquet of pink roses in his arms. "Hi, Ainsley."

She swallowed. "Uh, hi, Gage." Suddenly aware of her cleaning-day attire, her hand flew to snatch the bandanna off her hair. "Sorry. It's cleaning day and I wasn't expecting company."

"Don't worry about it. Besides, you always look beautiful to me." A small smile tilted his lips.

She gave him a sidelong glance. "Was that an attempt to get me to let you in?"

He shook his head. "No. Just the truth. Whether you let me in or not is up to you." He pointed past her. "If it were up to your neighbor there, I think she'd prefer we stay outside anyway."

Ainsley turned, and sure enough, Bebe was sitting on her porch, pretending to read a magazine. When Bebe saw Ainsley looking, she at least had the decency to raise the magazine higher, as if that's where she'd been looking all along. Ainsley rolled her eyes as she turned back toward Gage. "I love Bebe. She's a great neighbor, but the woman lives for gossip. So, come on inside."

"Thank God for nosy neighbors," Gage remarked as he entered the house.

She shut the door behind him. Gesturing toward the blooms in his arms, she asked, "Are those for me, or do you want me to call Cooper down?"

He laughed. "Guess I'm nervous. These are definitely for you." He handed them over.

"Thanks. I'll put them in the fridge until I can find a vase." She walked away to do that, then returned. "So, other than awkwardly giving me flowers, what brings you here?"

"Can we sit down and talk for a bit?"

She eyed him warily.

"I know I don't deserve it, but all I ask is that you give me a few minutes. Hear me out, and if at any time you get tired of listening, you can kick me out and I'll leave. No questions asked."

Her brain told her to tell him to kick rocks, but her heart was moved by the sincerity on his face. "Fair enough. Let's sit on the sofa."

They both sat, and she made sure to leave a good amount of space between them.

"I want to start by apologizing. I had no right to make judgments about your dating life or how you parent. And I'm sorry my attitude about children and fatherhood is so off-putting."

Wow. She'd never expected this level of self-awareness, and she had to admit it was refreshing. "Okay, I accept your apology."

"Great. I also need you to know that I'm seeking help. I don't really know why children make me uncomfortable, and I'm going to talk to a therapist about it so I can find out how to move forward in changing my attitudes."

"That's wonderful, Gage. It's also very evolved, because a lot of Black folks don't trust the validity of therapy." She watched him, saw the determination in his eyes. "You must really want to get to the bottom of this."

"I do." He reached for her hand, touching her gently. "I never took the time to really examine my feelings on fatherhood before, because I never had a strong enough reason. But now I do."

She frowned. "What's the reason?"

"You and Cooper." He squeezed her hand. "Ainsley, I want you in my life. Not as my assistant, but as my girlfriend. My lover. My confidante."

She felt the tears spring to her eyes. "Really?"

"Would I have made arrangements for 404 Sound to sponsor Cooper's baseball team if I wasn't serious about this?"

"Oh my gosh." She could already imagine how amped Coach Rigsby and the rest of the team would be to hear that.

"And would I have paid for three nonrefundable, all-inclusive tickets to Disney World for spring break?"

She pressed her palm to her chest. It was a lot to take in. "Oh wow. Those tickets cost a mint." Cooper had been asking her to go for a long time, and while she'd been saving up, it would have probably been another six or eight months before she had enough for a grand trip. Wiping the tears from her eyes, she asked, "What would you have done if I had turned you down?"

He shrugged. "I guess I would have taken Teagan and Miles, since they're basically kids. Wouldn't have been as much fun, though." He winked.

She blinked away a fresh set of tears. "I love you, Gage."

"I love you. And I promise to spend the rest of my life showing you it's real."

Gage pulled Ainsley into his arms, feeling a sweet relief spread through his body as he held her close. When he'd come here, he knew things could have gone either way. But he thanked his lucky stars that she'd been willing to listen and had been receptive to what he'd said.

He nudged her chin up, kissing her deeply. Their tongues mated and tangled for a few humid moments before she pulled back. "What's the matter? Shouldn't we be making up right now?"

"Absolutely. But remember, my child is right upstairs."

"Okay, so we'll kiss quietly." He drew her mouth

back to his again. As the kiss deepened, she leaned into him, and he held her tight against his heart.

He heard the sound of footsteps on the stairs and abruptly ended the kiss. They both turned their heads and saw an amused Cooper standing there on the last step, watching them.

"Hi, Cooper." Gage waved.

"Hi, Mr. Woodson." The youngster gave him a crooked half smile.

"You can call me Gage."

"Cool." Cooper turned his gaze to his mother. "Hey, Mom, does this mean you're not going to be looking sad anymore?"

Gage's eyes widened.

Ainsley, who'd turned five shades of red, smiled. "Yes, son. I'll be fine."

"Good." Cooper walked into the kitchen.

Ainsley looked at Gage and burst out laughing. Soon enough, he was laughing right along with her.

Cooper emerged from the kitchen and headed back up the steps, carrying a glass of water and an apple.

"Hey, Coop," Gage called out to him.

Cooper stopped. "What's up?"

"You seem like the type that looks out for his mom. That's a good thing. So, I'm giving you permission right now to beat me up if I ever make your mom cry again, okay?"

Cooper stared at him for a moment before saying,

"You got it." Then he went upstairs and disappeared around the corner.

Ainsley punched Gage in the shoulder. "Laying it on mighty thick, eh, Mr. Woodson?"

"Whatever I gotta do to keep you happy, I'm willing to do." He smiled. "It never hurts to have a contingency plan. If ever I think about stepping out of line, I'll just remember the beatdown I'm gonna catch from our kid."

Her big brown eyes grew even larger. "*Our* kid?"

He nodded. "You two are a package deal, as I understand it."

Her hands flew to her face.

He gently tugged her wrists. "Ainsley, I'll admit I don't know what I'm doing when it comes to kids. But what I do know is you've already given Cooper such a solid foundation. He's a good kid. Between working it out in therapy and watching you, I'm sure I can figure out how to be there for him, in whatever way you both need me to be."

Tears standing in her eyes, she looked wistfully at the top of the stairs. "He is a good kid. I'm so, so proud of him."

"And I'd be honored to be a part of his life." He squeezed her hands. "I know it's going to take time and effort, but I'm willing to put in the work."

She blew out a breath. "I really appreciate that, Gage."

"So…does this mean I'm forgiven, and we're a couple now?"

She laughed, nodding. "Oh yeah. You're stuck with us."

"Sounds great." He kissed each of her hands in turn. "I need to ask you something. It's still months away, but I don't want to wait till it's too late."

"What is it?"

"Will you be my date for the thirty-year anniversary gala? It's not until the fall."

She cringed. "Isn't it black-tie? I hate dressing up."

"I know. But it's only one night."

"Can I wear a nice pantsuit instead of some big poufy gown?"

"Sure." He knew his mom felt similarly about formal attire. "As a matter of fact, you're my mom's kindred spirit. She usually wears a tailored pantsuit. Says she hates being trapped in what she refers to as a 'taffeta prison.'"

She giggled. "Does your mom still do Krav Maga?"

"She does kickboxing now. She already got her green belt in Krav Maga."

"Your mom is my kindred spirit."

He smiled because seeing her this happy made him happy. "Since I'm here, and I'm interrupting your Sunday plans, why don't I help you clean?" He gestured to his jeans and short-sleeved blue polo. "I'm dressed for it."

"You don't have to ask twice. I never turn down housework help." She got up, handing him a microfiber cloth and a can of dusting spray. "You can start by dusting. Make sure you get the electronics, the windowsills and all the little collectibles on the mantelpiece."

Taking the items, he gave her a mock salute. "I'll get right on it, ma'am."

Shaking her head, she opened up the closet beneath the stairway and dragged out a huge vacuum cleaner.

Well into the afternoon, he helped her restore the house to neatness. They moved from the living room to the guest bedroom and half bath, then upstairs to the laundry room.

The last space they cleaned was her bedroom, and as they worked there, she showed him the family pictures she had on her wall of her mother and her favorite aunt, Eden's mother, Miriam.

"I don't know if it's okay to ask, but..."

"Where's my father? It's fine. He ran off when I was about three." She threw the last decorator pillow onto her freshly changed bed. "Cooper's father repeated the same behavior, so I guess now you can see why I'm cautious about who I date."

He nodded. "I understand, and you don't have to worry about that kind of bullshit from me."

Ainsley walked down the hall and into Cooper's room, with Gage close behind. "Looks clean in here. I think we're done. The whole place is spotless."

Back downstairs, the three of them had turkey sandwiches and chips for lunch, then piled on the couch to watch as Cooper played a fighting game on his console. Gage tried his hand at the game and promptly had his ass handed to him. What made it so bad was that while Gage frantically pressed buttons, trying to figure out how to land a hit or at least dodge the barrage of blows the kid dealt out, Cooper appeared as cool as the proverbial cucumber.

Cooper grinned. "Remember what you said earlier. Just know that if I come after you over Mom, it's not gonna be a game."

"I'm fully aware." Gage gave the kid a fist bump. "You're a fierce competitor, Coop."

"Usually only Mom and my friends call me that."

Gage cringed. *Is the kid about to lambaste me? Hasn't my ego suffered enough?*

Cooper laughed. "No worries. You can call me Coop."

And with that small acknowledgment, Gage felt like he'd taken his first big step in discovering the many facets of parenthood for himself.

Ainsley tapped her son on the shoulder. "Cooper, don't you have that book report to finish?"

He cringed, then nodded. "Yeah. It is due tomorrow."

"I've got an idea. Why don't you take your book and your notebook next door and let Bryce help you finish it up?"

Cooper looked thoughtful. "He did already finish his. And I think it will go faster if two of us work on it."

"Great." Ainsley pulled out her phone and texted Bebe. When Bebe responded a minute later, giving her permission for the boys to work together, she said, "Bebe's on board. Go ahead and gather up everything you need."

Under her watchful eye, Cooper gathered what he'd need into his book bag.

"After you finish your work, you can hang out for a while," Ainsley said as he headed for the door. "But you need to be back by six for dinner, okay?"

"Okay, Mom." With his book bag strap slung over one shoulder, Cooper left, closing the front door behind him.

Turning toward Gage, still seated on the couch, she said, "I seem to be child-free for a few hours."

Setting the remote aside, he met her gaze. "Then this seems like prime time for us to make up."

Laughing, she jogged up the stairs.

Gage gave chase and caught her in the doorway of her bedroom. Pulling her into his arms, he kissed her deeply. When they separated, he said, "You know I'm never letting you go again, right?"

"You won't be able to get rid of me." She tweaked his nose, then slid her hand down to his shirt collar, tugging him into her bedroom.

At the foot of the bed, she kicked off her bunny slippers and undid the three buttons at the collar of his polo. She stepped back, letting him take the shirt off while she tossed her own sweatshirt aside. They alternated between fevered kisses and removing articles of clothing until they were both nude. Then she let herself be pulled into his embrace. His muscled arms engulfed her, making her feel safe, loved.

Taking a step back, she sat on the bed. When he joined her, she straddled his lap, the mattress giving beneath their weight. He kissed her eyes, her cheeks, her lips. Then he slid his attentions to the hollow of her throat, the expert movements of his mouth making her head drop back from the heady pleasure.

He whispered into her neck, his breath warm against her damp skin. "Ride me, baby."

She raised herself and, with his large hands guiding her hips, sank onto his dick, purring as he filled her.

With a growl of his own, he moved his hands around to cup her ass.

She moved in slow, deliberate ways, rising and falling on his hardness in time with the passion glowing inside her. While her hips rocked, she pressed her lips against his, seeking the comfort of his kiss, a safe harbor in the raging storm.

He gripped her tighter and began lifting his hips to meet her stroke for stroke. Her core was on fire, ecstasy spreading from low in her belly until it reached the tips of her fingers and toes.

Ragged little cries escaped her throat as she got closer and closer to orgasm.

As if he could sense her state of mind, he wove his fingers into her curls and tugged her head until her ear was next to his mouth. "Come for me, baby. Let me hear you scream."

Moments later, she did just that. Her body flexed around his, her legs trembling with the force of the pleasure crashing over her.

He continued to pump until his own orgasm tore a growl from his lips.

Seventeen

Ainsley used her key tag to unlock the door to the resort suite, then held it open so Cooper could enter. She followed him in, with Gage close behind. They'd had an amazing, fun-filled day at Epcot, and while she was utterly exhausted, she was also smiling from ear to ear.

While Cooper ran off to use the bathroom, she flopped onto the sofa in the main part of their two-bedroom suite. "I don't know about you, but I'm beat."

Gage blew out a breath as he sat down next to her. "Same. Where do kids get all that energy from?"

She shrugged. "Some of it came from sugar. As for the rest, I wish I knew. If I could harness it,

I wouldn't need coffee anymore." She heard the sound of the toilet flushing, then water running.

Cooper appeared a few moments later. "Mom, can I—"

"Oh, honey. Please don't tell me you want another snack. Or that you want to go anywhere else tonight."

He shook his head. "No. I know we usually play board games in the evening, but I was gonna ask if I could just go to bed. I'm really tired."

Her brow hitched. "Oh. Well, that's fine. Just come over and kiss me good-night first."

"Aw, Mom." He trudged over to her, leaned down and gave her a peck on the cheek. "Love you, Mom."

"I love you, too."

Turning to Gage, he gave him a double fist bump, which had become their customary greeting over the last several weeks. "Good night, Gage."

Gage winked at him. "'Night, champ."

Cooper went to his bedroom and closed the door behind him. She could hear him moving around inside the room for a few minutes, probably changing into his pajamas. Soon, though, the light flipped off and the room went silent.

"Hey. Let's go sit out on the balcony for a little bit." Gage squeezed her shoulder, brushing his lips against her cheek.

"Sounds nice. I'll grab us a couple of glasses of wine."

Soon, they were seated on the cushioned wicker love seat on the room's balcony, enjoying the warm night air and the view. From their tenth-floor room, they had a great view of the dimly lit, manicured landscaping around the resort. Their room also offered a view of the nearby lagoon, and while she sipped from her glass of merlot, Ainsley watched a flock of geese gliding over the glassy surface of the water.

"It's beautiful out here."

"You're right about that." He raised his arm, placing it around her shoulders. "Gorgeous scenery, gorgeous company."

She smiled. "Very sly, Gage."

He took her glass, setting it down on the glass-topped table next to the love seat along with his own. "I meant every word, and you know it."

She gave him a peck on the cheek. "I know."

"I have something important I want to say."

She looked into his eyes, feeling herself drown in the liquid brown pools. "I'm listening."

"Ainsley, spending all this time with you has been amazing. But to tell you the truth, I expected that. What I didn't expect was how much I'd come to care about Cooper."

She felt herself grinning. "You two have really been getting along well. When you're not around, he talks about you. I know he really likes you."

"I'm glad to hear that. I feel like Cooper and I have bonded." He swatted a mosquito about to make a meal of his forearm. "Dr. Vance has really helped me work through a lot of my issues pertaining to children, and he says that my budding relationship with Cooper is helping my progress immensely."

"That's great. I'm so glad to hear it's going well." She took a deep breath. "Because I have something to tell you."

"And I'd love to hear it. Just let me say this first. I could tell Cooper was a good kid. But the more I get to know him, the more I want to be a part of his life. As he gets older, he'll need some male guidance, and I want to be there for him." He squeezed her hand. "Now, what were you going to tell me?"

She chewed her lip for a moment. "Remember the day you showed up with those flowers, and we went upstairs to make love?"

He chuckled. "Of course, I remember."

"Well, do you remember that we were so hot for each other that we didn't use protection?"

He paused. "Wait a minute." His eyes darted from her eyes to her belly, then back again. "Are you… could you be…"

"Pregnant?" She teased, finishing his sentence. "Very."

His grin seemed to show every last one of his permanent teeth. "Ainsley. Baby, that's amazing. You're amazing." He laid his palm over her belly, which barely showed any evidence of the life growing inside her. "I'm gonna take such good care of you. I promise."

"You're not nervous?" She hadn't known how he'd

react to the news, especially considering the way he'd struggled around children in the past.

"Not at all. I'm working through the things I need to work through so I can be a great father. Not only to Cooper, but to our baby as well."

He looks so damn earnest. She could feel her eyes welling up. "Damn it, Gage. Why do you have to be so wonderful?"

"You ain't seen nothing yet, baby." He reached into the pocket of his short-sleeved button-down shirt and pulled out a small black box. Dropping to one knee in front of her, he said, "This isn't just about Cooper. It's about you, and all the ways you make my life better. I've loved you for so long, and when you finally gave me a chance, I almost ruined everything." He flipped open the box, showing her the two-carat princess-cut solitaire inside. "Now that I've got you back, I don't ever want to be without you again. Ainsley Elaine Voss, will you marry me?"

A sob broke forth from her lips, tears coursing down her face. She wanted to say yes, but she couldn't talk and sob at the same time, so she stuck out her hand and nodded furiously.

"Is that a yes? I need to hear it from you."

Taking a few deep, steadying breaths, she finally found her voice and shouted, "Yes!"

Grinning, he placed the ring on her finger and tossed the box aside.

She leaned in for his kiss, and the moment their lips connected, she felt her heart swell with affection. He made her feel alive in a way no one else ever had. In the last two months, he'd shown her a love she never would have expected to find, especially not after motherhood began to dominate her life.

A loud popping sound scared her, causing her to break the kiss. Looking to the sky, she saw the source of the sound as thousands of sparkly, multicolored points of light painted the sky. It was one of the park's famous nightly fireworks shows, and it was beautiful.

But as far as Ainsley was concerned, nothing could match the fireworks she felt inside.

Sitting at his desk, Gage stifled a yawn as he looked over the previous month's operations report. It was a Monday, and he'd just come back from an amazing vacation with Ainsley and Cooper. It was the least motivated he'd felt to be at work in a long time, but there were still things to be done, so he pressed on.

He took a sip from his now tepid coffee as he flipped the page on the report. A soft tapping sound drew his attention, and he looked up to see Ainsley standing in his office door. She wore a black knee-length shirtdress that showed off the length of her honey-brown legs. "Can I come in?"

"By all means." He slid his chair back from the desk, inviting her to sit on his lap.

She giggled. "Now, Mr. Woodson, we're at work.

That wouldn't be appropriate professional behavior, would it?"

"We're engaged, baby." He rolled his eyes but didn't lose his smile. "You're gonna get enough of teasing me about that one day."

She sidled around his desk and sat on his lap. "Okay. I just wanted to stop by before I left for the meeting and get a good-luck kiss."

He wrapped his arms around her, happy to oblige her request. When she broke the kiss a few minutes later, she said, "I'll have to redo my lipstick, since you're wearing it all now."

Grabbing a napkin from the top drawer of his desk, he wiped his mouth. "You look beautiful, as always. Now go over there and see what they have to say. You said your first two interviews went well."

She got up, straightening the hem of her dress. "They did, and I have a good feeling. But there's a lot of competition for the HR position. You know, if I get the job, you're going to have to replace me as your assistant."

"You're a tough act to follow, babe. But I've got my eye on a few candidates from the intern pool downstairs." He shooed her out. "Don't worry about that. Just go and be amazing."

She blew him a kiss as she headed out. "I love you."

"I love you, too, sugar."

While she was gone, he went about his workday. He finished going over the operations report, signed off on it and emailed it to Nia's assistant to be archived. With that done, he left his office and went down to the first floor to check in on the recording session in Studio 1.

Inside the control room, he sat next to Teagan, who was working the Digital Audio Workstation. The baby of the family and younger twin to his brother Miles, Teagan's official title was chief technology officer. In her heart, however, she was a sound engineer. On any given workday, she was far more likely to be found in the studio than in her office on the fourth floor.

Putting the final touches on his album, The Visionary was in the booth, sitting on a stool jotting notes on a pad, but already wearing headphones.

"Where's the production team?"

"They were here Friday and said they'd drop back by at the end of this week to check on his progress." Teagan gestured to the artist. "He's a pretty independent worker, and he writes on his feet. All I've really been doing is giving him playback to riff on."

"Good." He spent a few more moments watching the artist as he wrote, then asked, "So, sis. After two months, do you still like the new equipment?"

Teagan's grin broadened. "Gage, this workstation is awesome. I'm discovering new things every day. The features on this thing are great, and it's making my job a whole lot easier." She rested her cheek on the surface of the workstation. "I've named her Fancy."

Gage laughed. "Jeez, Teagan. You're such a nerd."

"I know, but in my line of work it comes in handy." She winked. "Now, get out of my studio. I don't want you making our artist nervous."

Standing, Gage glanced at The Visionary, thinking he should stop in and say hello. But seeing how deep the lyricist was in his writing process, he decided not to bother him. Tipping an imaginary hat toward his baby sister, he returned to his office to get some more work done.

Just before lunch, Ainsley returned, and when he looked up and saw the broad grin on her face, he knew what she was about to say. He stood up. "You got the job?"

"Yes!" She nearly screamed the answer, her excitement apparent. "I start as human resources manager next Monday. I'll have my own office, and get this, I get an assistant, too!"

He pulled her into his arms. "Congratulations, baby! I'm so proud of you."

"Thank you." She pecked him on the lips. "Now, I have to ask. You didn't interfere in the process, right?"

He shook his head. "Absolutely not. You forbade me to get involved, and I don't want to end up on your bad side. Cooper will end me."

She laughed. "Well, I'm happy to know you followed my wishes."

"How about a celebratory lunch?"

"Sounds wonderful."

He grabbed his wallet and keys and followed his beautiful bride-to-be out the door.

Eighteen

When the plane had raised its wheels and carried her away from Summer Village, Louisiana, four months back, Ainsley had no reason to believe she'd ever return to the quaint little town. Yet today, it seemed only right that she and Gage return to the place where they'd finally succumbed to their feelings for each other.

Standing by the mirror in a downstairs room of the inn, she checked her appearance one more time. She smoothed her hands over the flowing skirt of the knee-length white sundress she'd chosen for this occasion. The skirt left plenty of room for her expanding waistline, without sacrificing style. The halter neck was accentuated by tiny embroidered pink rosettes, and she'd swept her hair up into a messy bun.

Eden appeared then, tucking a fresh pink rose and a sprig of baby's breath into her cousin's hair. "You look beautiful, Ainsley."

"Thanks, E." With one final glance in the mirror, she said, "I think I'm ready."

"Then let's get you married."

Riding with Eden in the rented sedan, she held her sequined white clutch and watched the scenery passing by. The familiarity of the place touched her, and she knew then that returning to this place for their special day had been the right choice. *Maybe we should come here for our anniversary every few years.*

They arrived at Simmons Lake Park, and as Eden parked the car, Ainsley took in the sight of the gathering with a smile. Down by the lake, an old gazebo stood, which was now festooned with crepe paper wedding bells and streamers. She crossed the grass, her arm linked with Eden's. Inside the gazebo stood the local justice of the peace, and Gage stood next to him. The sight of her husband-to-be made the tears start gathering in her eyes. Gage looked handsome in his white shirt, tan slacks and brown loafers. Next to him stood Cooper, in a matching outfit. A pink rose boutonniere was pinned to each of their collars.

A grouping of about twenty chairs was set up, and as Ainsley walked down the white runner aisle, she glanced around at the faces of the Redford family, the Woodsons and a few of their colleagues from work. She felt her smile growing wider.

Beneath the gazebo and the canopy of trees, she

and Gage exchanged their vows. Her hands trembled as he placed the white-gold band on her finger. And when the justice of the peace pronounced them married, Gage pulled her into his arms, leaned her back and kissed her as if no one was watching.

After the ceremony, they convened at the Blue Rose for refreshments. Sitting on Gage's lap at their table in the center of the diner, Ainsley said, "This day has been perfect in every way."

"I'm glad to hear that."

"I love it here." She sighed contentedly.

"Oh, so would you rather I cancel those tickets to Egypt and we can just spend our honeymoon here instead?"

She cut her eyes at him. "Nah. I need to see the pyramids."

His eyes took on a wicked gleam. "And I need to see how many ways I can make you scream on another continent."

She punched him in the shoulder. "You're too much, Gage."

"But I'm just right for you." He gave her hip an affectionate squeeze. "I love you, Ainsley Voss-Woodson."

She responded with all the love she felt inside. "And I love you, Gage."

* * * * *

*Wealthy Alaskan Cash Outlaw has inherited a ranch and
needs land owned by beautiful, determined
Brianna Banks. She'll sign it over under one condition:
Cash fathering the child she desperately wants. But he
won't be an absentee father and makes his own demand...*

Read on for a sneak peek at
The Marriage He Demands
by New York Times *bestselling author Brenda Jackson.*

"Are you really going to sell the Blazing Frontier without
even taking the time to look at it? It's a beautiful place."

"I'm sure it is, but I have no need of a ranch, dude or
otherwise."

"I think you're making a mistake, Cash."

Cash lifted a brow. Normally, he didn't care what any
person, man or woman, thought about any decision he made,
but for some reason what she thought mattered.

It shouldn't.

What he should do was thank her for joining him for
lunch, and tell her not to walk back to Cavanaugh's office
with him, although he knew both their cars were parked there.
In other words, he should put as much distance between them
as possible.

I can't.

Maybe it was the way her luscious mouth tightened when
she was not happy about something. He'd picked up on it
twice now. Lord help him but he didn't want to see it a third
time. He'd rather see her smile, lick an ice cream cone or...
lick him.

He quickly forced the last image from his mind, but not before a hum of lust shot through his veins. There had to be a reason he was so attracted to her. Maybe he could blame it on the Biggins deal Garth had closed just months before he'd gotten engaged to Regan. That had taken working endless days and nights, and for the past year Cash's social life had been practically nonexistent.

On the other hand, even without the Biggins deal as an excuse, there was strong sexual chemistry radiating between them. He felt it but honestly wasn't sure that even at twenty-seven she recognized it for what it was.

That was intriguing, to the point that he was tempted to hang around Black Crow another day. Besides, he was a businessman, and no businessman would sell or buy anything without checking it out first. He was letting his personal emotions around Ellen cloud what was usually a very sound business mind.

"You are right, Brianna. I would be making a mistake if I didn't at least see the ranch before selling it. Is now a good time?"

The huge smile that spread across her face was priceless… and mesmerizing. When was the last time a woman, any woman, had this kind of effect on him? When he felt spellbound? He concluded that never had a woman captivated him like Brianna Banks was doing.

Don't miss what happens next in
The Marriage He Demands
by Brenda Jackson, the next book in her
Westmoreland Legacy: The Outlaws series!

Available April 2021 wherever
Harlequin Desire books and ebooks are sold.

Harlequin.com

HDEXP0321

Get 4 FREE REWARDS!

We'll send you 2 FREE Books plus 2 FREE Mystery Gifts.

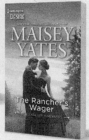

Harlequin Desire books transport you to the world of the American elite with juicy plot twists, delicious sensuality and intriguing scandal.

FREE Value Over $20
